Mine to Covet

Veteran K9 Team
Book 5

Kameron Claire

Snuggle Whore Press, LLC

Copyright © 2024 by Kameron Claire

All rights reserved.

No part of this book may be reproduced in any form or by any electronic or mechanical means, including information storage and retrieval systems, without written permission from the author, except for the use of brief quotations in a book review.

This is a work of fiction. Names, characters, places, and incidents either are the products of the author's imagination or are used fictitiously based upon freely provided by fan submission. Any resemblance to actual persons, living or dead, businesses, companies, events, or locales is entirely coincidental.

Please respect the author and do not participate in or encourage piracy of copyrighted materials that would violate the author's rights.

Contains explicit love scenes and adult language. The suggested reading audience is 18 years or older.

Editor: Shay M Williams

Covers by SWP Covers

Dedication

This series is dedicated to every individual
who signs a blank check on their ass
by enlisting in the Armed Forces
to serve their country—and to the
loved ones who support them back home.

We are Witty, Wicked & Wild wherever we go!

VETERAN
K9
TEAM
REPORTING
FOR DUTY

Chapter 1
Logan

I roll up to a collection of metal structures that serve more function than aesthetic, the sound of a dozen dogs at play in the distance creating an ambiance that the buildings lack. The wind is wild on the plain today, playing havoc on a collection of workers setting up a giant tent to the south of the building.

In the far distance, the mountain range offers a breathtakingly beautiful backdrop.

We are east of Spring City.

East of civilization.

East of clean air, I think, as a plume of dust kicks up and dances across the shiny black hood of my rented BMW.

I knew I should have rented a 4x4.

Not that I'm a priss. I've lived in the muck just like my brethren inside these buildings, but that doesn't mean I don't enjoy the finer things.

Always have, always will.

That's why they call me Hollywood—because even when I'm dirty, I shine.

Actually, they call me Hollywood because a few of them think they know where my money comes from, but the rest of them do it because of the first reason since I never talk about my familial connections. Most of the guys I've served with wouldn't believe I'm the youngest brother of a famous actor, an Academy Award-winning director, a top-rated stuntman, or an international super-model—even though we all look alike. We're third-generation film and television—the epitome of silver screen glitz and glamor. My father is an executive with Mejers Studios, the company my great-grandfather started in 1936. His granddaughter, my mother, was a horror queen in the eighties.

Loosely translated, I'm Hollywood royalty, except I left it all behind the day I swore into the US Army—much to my mother's embarrassment.

"Dude? Did I lose you?" Levi's—my brother, the stuntman—voice comes over the car audio.

"No, man. Sorry." I shake my head, clearing the looming dread trying to settle in my chest. It's weird, but I'm more nervous about going home to see my family than I have ever been deploying to an active warzone.

"So, pick you up at the airport on Monday, yeah?"

"I can take a car."

"That's rubbish, mate."

I chuckle. "Rubbish, eh? Still dating Australian models?"

"I'm in between girlfriends at the moment." He

pauses. "I'm glad you're coming home, Logan. It'll be good to spend time with you. I've missed you."

Fuck. Why does the wild and crazy brother have to be the most sentimental? "I've missed you, too. I'll send you my flight information and see you at the airport around eleven on Monday."

"Cool. See you then."

Turning off the engine, I take a deep breath and send up a silent prayer that this business opportunity gives me the purpose and direction I desperately need after I separate from the military. My family thinks I'm coming back to Beverly Hills, but that's the last thing I want to do.

I walk through the front door of the Veteran K9 Center, half expecting the floor to be dirt, but am surprised by a thick pad of stained concrete with paw prints artfully stamped in decorative lines to multiple end-points. The inside is eerily quiet, but I can hear the dogs beyond the metal building in the outdoor kennels or training area.

Is this the business I'll buy into?

I trust the guys who turned me on to this place— Karden and Saint—and knew their dogs when we deployed together, but is this the best use of my trust fund?

"Hollywood." Karden and Kiki come out of a back office. The brute is even bigger than I remember. It's been five months since I last saw him, but his Belgian Malinois runs up to me like it was yesterday.

I bend down and lean my head forward, letting her sniff my hair before she climbs up and puts her paws on my shoulders, simultaneously knocking me on my ass. I'm not a K9 handler like the rest of them—just a guy in a flak vest with an M-4 strapped across my chest, taking long walks through eerily desolate streets. Unlike some of the men I served with, I'm only doing six years in the military—one enlistment—and honestly, it's enough.

After watching a friend die less than two feet from me earlier this year while another bled with his own bullet wound, I knew I wasn't going to re-up.

Don't get me wrong, my military time was worth it because I met guys like the one standing in front of me wearing a shit-eating grin on his handsome face. Training and deploying to remote locations grounded me in a way that Hollywood, Beverly Hills, Pacific Palisades, and Malibu never could—and taught me life lessons I wouldn't have learned otherwise.

Most of these guys came from somewhere between lower-middle class and pure poverty, where I was born with a literal silver pacifier in my mouth. It was the ulti-mate act of rebellion for me to enter the military after high school instead of going to the Ivy League university bought and paid for by my mother. Serving my country wasn't her problem, (well, not her only problem), but doing it as an enlisted man—the lowest of the low—blem-ished her perfect reputation.

What am I supposed to tell the paparazzi, Logan?

Of course, the family tried to spin it into a Holly-wood-worthy tale by turning me into a war hero before I ever stepped foot into boot camp, but I had a PR team bury that noise as quickly as it surfaced. I've done everything I can to remain invisible—the forgotten Mejer son.

I'm no one special—just another grunt with a job to do. With that phase of my life approaching an end, I want to do something with my trust fund that means something.

I want to do many meaningful somethings.

Now that I've turned twenty-five, the only thing left for me to do is go home, sign the paperwork, and release the funds into my accounts.

"Jesus, look at the size of that melon." I grin up from the floor at Karden who, despite his good looks, gives off a hardened criminal vibe with all of his black and gray tattoos.

He offers me his hand and yanks me to my feet, pulling me into a one-armed bear hug. "Good to see you, Hollywood. Have you ETS'd yet?"

"January tenth is the official date, but I hope to be moving before the new year. I'm on leave this week, and then I'll head back to final out."

"Do you think you'll come here?" He cocks his brow. While he might have been the one to introduce me to his boss, Janey LaVey, he's not in the know as to the depths of our discussions. Janey is ex-military like everyone else at the Veteran K9 Center, and although we were active at the same time, our paths never crossed. The only thing I know about her are rumors—dark, disturbing stories that would make any decent man's blood boil. I know the guys are protective of her and this place is family for all of them.

So yeah, of course, I'm drawn to this location. At least two of these guys are already like brothers.

I shrug. "We'll see."

"It would be good to have you nearby." He chucks me on the shoulder and then leads me into the back offices where one guy sits at a computer while two others pack their go-bags. There are three more dogs in this space—a German Shepherd and two Huskies.

"Hey guys. This is Logan—" Karden introduces me to the room "—but you might hear me slip up and call him Hollywood from time to time."

"Holy shit, man. What the fuck are you doing here?" Lincoln Abrams—a guy I went through boot camp with—grins, drops his bag, and offers me his hand.

I clasp palms with him and grin. "I'm here to check out the facility."

"You're the investor?" His jaw drops a little. "God-damn. I guess the rumors were true."

I put on a well-practiced blank expression and give him a noncommittal shrug, diverting the topic as soon as it comes up, like I've always done. I guess eventually I'll have to come clean with these people, especially if we get into business together, but today is not that day.

"Man, I thought you went pararescue, not K9." I can't believe Lincoln is here right now. I've known a ton of adrenaline junkies in my lifetime—most of them work as stuntmen on big blockbusters or as bodyguards for A-list celebrities—and Lincoln rivals them all.

He shakes his head. "That is also a long story. One I don't have time to tell."

"Yeah, we've got to get up to the mountain and get clocked in." The other guy offers me his hand. "Barron Theroux."

"Sergeant Major Theroux? Damn, I've heard of you."

Holy shit. He trained these guys—but I never had the pleasure of meeting the man. Looks like this place is thick with men who have solid reputations. That's a plus in the pros and cons tally I'm keeping in my head while weighing my potential investment.

Lincoln hauls his backpack up on his shoulder and nods. "We work search and rescue at Silver Mountain Ski Resort two weekends a month. Occasionally we take on ski instruction, but only if the lodge bunny is super hot."

The salacious spread of his lips and waggle of his brow has me shaking my head. If I remember correctly, he was a self-proclaimed player at eighteen, too. "You haven't changed one bit."

"Hell, no. Why mess with perfection?"

Barron snorts and heads out with the old German Shepherd following him, her hips aching if the way she has to work to get up off the floor is any sign. "We'll see you guys Monday."

One Husky sidles up to Lincoln's side as he also turns to leave. "Grab my number from Karden. If you're still in town on Sunday night, let's grab a drink."

I nod. "Sounds good."

We bump fists, and I finally get a chance to make eye contact with the third man in the room, his hair and thick beard a dark brown. He stands and offers his hand. "John Vale."

"Damn. I've heard of you, too." I shake his hand.

"Is that a good or bad thing?" He chuckles.

"It's impressive. It means Ms. LaVey has assembled an all-star team."

"Yeah," Karden interjects, "and as long as Saint separates in March like he's supposed to, he has a job waiting for him, too."

"He mentioned he was coming. Between the two of you, I've been getting an earful for the last four months." I turn around as the front doors open and close, male and female voices rising above the din.

"Whose BMW is parked out front?" An enormous man with biceps the size of my head says before he enters the room, his eyes coming to me. "I guess it's yours. Nice ride."

I shrug. "It's a rental."

"You must be Logan. I'm Michael, but everyone calls me Kemp."

I shake his hand and turn to the petite yet muscular woman behind him. "And you must be Ms. LaVey."

She frowns and shakes her head. "Janey, please. No one calls me Miss anything, although if you must, you can call me LaVey. I'll probably answer out of pure habit."

I chuckle lightly and look away, disturbed by the faded scars on her left cheek. I guess the rumors are true. Fucking bastard. "It's nice to meet you, Janey."

"Come with me." She motions for me to follow, a massive Rottweiler trailing behind her.

I glance at Karden and Vale. "I'll see you guys around."

"Yeah, man. We'll have dinner tonight," Karden says.

I nod. "Works for me."

Kemp follows me into a makeshift conference/break room and closes the door behind us. "Do you want coffee, tea, water, soda, beer?"

"I'm good. Thanks."

Janey unrolls a couple of giant sheets of paper, spreading them out over the table. "I appreciate you flying in today."

"And I appreciate you staying late to meet with me. I'm flying to Southern California on Monday to see the family for Thanksgiving and handle some paperwork, and then I have to get back to Fort Lewis to start my out-processing."

"And then you're a free man," Kemp adds.

I shrug. "Let's see if we can negotiate where my next home will be."

Janey sighs. "We'll cut to the chase, then. I have some rough sketches of what we want to build here, and while I would have loved to razzle-dazzle you with professional blueprints and 3D models, to be honest, we can't afford the pretties just yet. We're operating in the black, but just barely, and giving those guys in the other room pay raises is my priority after taking care of the dogs."

"You've assembled a good team. Their reputations precede them. I'm impressed."

She smiles and exchanges a look with Kemp. "Yeah, we're lucky they will work for dog food."

That makes me chuckle.

She continues. "The road you came in on is actually a

back road, but if we build a new facility, we would turn these buildings into kennels and an indoor play area. The new building would be best situated here—" she points to a spot on the map west of the current facility "—which would provide better access to our high-traffic customers. It would equip the facility with more of a storefront versus a collection of old hay barns in the middle of nowhere."

"And the twenty acres west of you?" We've talked about this a lot via email.

She sighs. "I've been haggling with the owners for months, but they won't budge on their number. As I told you via email, I think they are holding out for a housing developer, which will cause us nothing but grief if they build close to our facility."

"Yeah, they'll complain about the dogs barking on day one," I agree.

Kemp nods. "Any properties built out here will be million-dollar homes, and the last thing they want to over-look from their breakfast nooks are a bunch of working dogs and big meatheads running around in giant padded suits."

I chuckle. "That would be a sight to wake up to."

Janey flips over the aerial map to a rough sketch of a building divided up into multiple rooms or sections. "As you know, our core mission is to take care of military members and their four-legged furbabies. We're not looking to make money off of soldiers or airmen kenneling their animals while they are deployed or away at school. The potential for decent profit comes from training military-grade service animals, specifically for the local law enforcement agencies. Kemp and I have spent the last two years cultivating relationships with some of the canine officers in Spring City, and are working to get our hooks into the guys up in Denver. We've also gotten ourselves certified to train PTSD service animals for military veterans. Did you notice the tents outside?"

"I was going to ask you about those."

She nods. "That's why I felt it was important you come out this weekend. We've been busting our asses to coordinate the first Paws for a Cause animal fundraiser at our facility. One of the local shelters will bring a dozen or more animals for adoption, and we will showcase our training, kenneling, and service animal program."

"That's smart." I nod.

"We will give a portion of the donations to the animal shelter, but a bulk of it will go toward training the first couple of dogs for our new PTSD program, which will be free to qualifying veterans."

Janey points to the different rooms in this large, public-facing building. "For tomorrow, we've set up a little craft fair, inviting canine-focused vendors. The idea is—and this is where the true revenue via passive income comes in—we'd create and lease space to individual business owners. A groomer here, a physical therapist there, a dog bakery here, a toy and treat cart there. Maybe even an on-site vet clinic."

Kemp nods. "An on-site veterinarian is the dream."

"We'd maintain the building, utilities, et cetera, and rent out space to entrepreneurs who can run their small businesses. We've done some rough market research and have assembled a list of current booth and room rental rates in Spring City. I'm not a business expert, but I think the investment in a building, advertising, and everything related could be profitable within two years."

"Maybe three," Kemp adds.

I nod, thinking more to myself. I'm not a business expert either, but I trust my gut and it's telling me that while this won't be nearly as profitable as throwing my money at a hedge fund wheeling and dealing real estate, stocks, and commodities, this is an effort that will feed my soul and my pocketbook. "What does my involvement look like besides financier?"

She shrugs. "I guess we'd need to figure that out. I'm willing to hear your thoughts on it."

"Well, considering I don't know dick about dogs outside of the fact that I've always wanted one, I'm thinking I will keep my nose out of the current business and focus on land, new build, and legalities of being a commercial landlord. The first thing I have to do is buy the twenty acres, and then we need to meet with lawyers and architects, and find ourselves a good general contractor."

"Just like that?" Janey looks from me to Kemp and back again. "You don't want to take a few weeks to think about it?"

I shrug. "I go with my gut a lot, and after next week, I'll have a stupid amount of money in my accounts. I can invest in this, which I believe will feed my soul, and still live comfortably. Plus, I'd like to be part of something bigger than myself, and I think this is it."

Offering her my hand, I flash her an easy smile. "What do you think? Can we be business partners?"

She shakes my hand. "Partners."

I follow Karden and Kiki to the Last Stand, a roadside country bar along Highway 24 between the VKC and Spring City. It's a little after seven, and after a long day of travel, I could use a drink.

"Is this the local haunt?" I ask, walking next to Karden with Kiki by his side.

"Yeah. We rarely come here with the dogs on weekends, just to avoid any drama. But it's early enough that I think it will be okay."

"What do you think of living in Spring City?" I've been here less than an hour, but I hope to take the weekend to explore and get my bearings.

"I like it here. It's the perfect cross of big city commerce and small mountain town vibes. Both busy and laid back at the same time. The Rangers, our local football team, is ranked number one in the league. We have enough active and retired military here to be comfortable, a state university, and an international airport within seventy miles. The weather is pretty awesome, and even when it's cold, it's not cold for long." He shrugs. "I think you'd like it here."

We take two seats at the bar. "I'm hoping so..."

The bartender walks out of the back with a bucket of ice, and I'm struck speechless at the vision before me. My chest constricts as all the air evaporates from my lungs. Standing in front of us is the most beautiful woman I have ever seen in my twenty-five years on this earth, and I was raised around curated glamor and ageless beauty.

Dark, nearly black hair falls in long, luscious waves around her bare, tattooed shoulders. She's wearing a black and purple bustier that barely contains her full breasts and delicious curves—the overt sexiness of her top downplayed by a pair of well-worn jeans slung low on her hips, which makes the total package no less sexy.

She sets the lip of the ice bucket on the trough and brings her gray eyes up to mine. Electricity skitters down my spine and jump starts my heart. Any questions I had about my next move after separating from the military dissipates.

My future is looking at me, and she's here in Spring City.

VETERAN
K9
TEAM
REPORTING
FOR DUTY

Chapter 2
Tess

"Hey girl!" I call to Jamie as she walks through the side door used by employees and band members. She waves back and holds up a finger, letting me know she'll be by shortly. Usually, we chat as the band sets up their equipment, and while the crowd is still sparse.

Working as a bartender at the Last Stand was not on my career dream list in high school, but it pays decently, the clientele is chill yet diverse enough as to not be boring, and I'm only doing this until the day I can afford to run my doggie bakery full-time.

It's my dream of dreams, which probably means I'll be tending bar into my sixties.

Heading to the ice machine in the back, I fill a five-pound bucket and lug it to the front to find two hotties taking a seat at the end of my bar. One of them I've seen a few times, usually accompanied by two or more other hotties and their dogs, but the blond next to him is new and infinitely better looking than all the other guys combined.

I mean, I don't think any of them get kicked out of bed, but this guy has movie-star looks.

Too beautiful for Spring City.

Way too beautiful for the Last Stand Saloon.

He brings his green eyes up to mine and something inside me combusts, freezing me in place as I miss the container and dump almost half of the ice on top of my boots.

"Fuck!" I stop pouring and take a step back, embarrassment painting my cheeks red.

He grins. "You okay?"

"Yeah, yeah." I wave him off and scurry back into the kitchen, cursing my life.

Marcus, our line cook, raises his brow. "Are you okay?"

"I need a shovel so I can clean ice off the ground."

He snickers and walks out to survey the damage, yelling back at me in my hiding space in the kitchen. "What the fuck did you do, girlie?"

"Shut up," I yell back.

"How are you doing?" I hear Marcus say before he returns to the kitchen with a shit-eating grin on his face. "I see the distraction."

I roll my eyes, a snow shovel in my hand.

He snatches it from me. "Go take care of every gay man and straight woman's dream while I clean up your mess."

I give him a thirty-second head start, straighten my

shoulders, and tilt up my chin. One of my superpowers is pretending like everything is fine - great - grand despite evidence to the contrary. Skirting the slippery mess, I grab a stack of coasters and slap two down in front of them. "What can I get you?"

Green Eyes' gaze is unwavering as he catalogs every freckle on my face—not that I have many. "What do you have on tap that's local?"

Shrugging, I wave toward the taps, unable to take my eyes off of him. "They're pretty much all Colorado-based breweries."

"Which one is your favorite?"

I sigh and glance over my shoulder at the taps again. "When I drink beer, I prefer a winter porter or stout."

"I'll take that."

The other guy nods. "Two, please. And a couple of menus."

I smack my hand on the bar, pretending to be completely unaffected by Green Eyes, and turn on my heel. "You got it."

Staying out of Marcus's way as he cleans up my mess, I slide a couple of menus in front of them and try not to notice the intensity coming off of the one guy. He's wearing a small smile, authentic enough not to be creepy, subdued enough to not come across as goofy. It's filled with knowledge, as if he already knows what he wants without looking at the menu.

Weirdly enough, I'm pretty sure he thinks it's me.

It should creep me out.

Let me be clear, it doesn't.

Still, I'm not going to make it easy on him.

As I'm pouring their beers, I hear Jamie chirp with excitement behind me. "What are you doing here?"

I turn to find her talking to the second guy, the one with dark blond hair, a square jaw, and multiple tattoos. Considering my ink, you'd think he'd be the one I'm attracted to instead of the clean slate starlet—the one with a boyish charm darkened only by real-world knowledge. He could play the hot boy next door or tortured artist in my fantasies and would rock either role.

The guy with the tattoos shrugs. "Grabbing a bite with my buddy and checking out the band."

"You know we're going to be at the center tomorrow afternoon?" Jamie smiles at me and points to the guy she is talking to as I set down their beers. "This is Karden. He is one of the guys that trains Nanook."

I arch my brow. "You work at the VKC?" Even though I've seen these guys with their service dogs many times, I've never actually talked to any of them.

He nods. "I do."

"I'm Logan." The other guy interjects and offers me his hand.

"Tess." His handshake is firm, but not overpowering, as if he wants to make sure we're connecting without performing some kind of flex. I have to admit, I appreciate a firm handshake. "Are you a K9 trainer too?"

"Not exactly."

"Come say hi to my husband, Kirian." Jamie slaps Karden on the shoulder, pulling him off his stool and leaving me with Logan.

"Alone at last." He grins before taking a draw of his beer.

"Is that what you were hoping for?"

"Absolutely."

"And why is that?"

"How else am I going to capture your undivided attention while my big, bad friend is sitting next to me?"

I place my hands on my hips and throw him a sassy smile. "Are you afraid he's better looking than you?"

He shakes his head. "I know he's not."

"That's a mighty cocky statement, considering he is a good-looking guy."

"As my friend Saint says—not cocky, confident."

"Oh? And what are you confident about?"

"That I'm the man you've been waiting for."

I roll my eyes. "Oh my god. Get me some tortilla chips, Marcus, because the cheese is thick over here."

Logan chuckles. "I wish I could buy you a drink."

"Well, it so happens this is the one place where the owners don't mind if I share a drink with a customer while working."

"Line us up two of whatever you want."

"Whatever I want?" I arch my brow. "You realize I can grab a bottle of the most expensive whiskey we have and take your credit card for a ride with that open statement?"

He shrugs. "I'm positive you're worth it."

I don't grab the most expensive whiskey we have, but instead mix us up a couple of shooters. A minute later, I'm setting down the two shots in front of him.

"What's this?" he asks.

"Screaming orgasm."

He barely controls the smile taking over his face as he sniffs it, his eyes locking onto mine. "To new friends and special beginnings."

I clink my shot glass against his and down it, tapping the empty glass against the bar top.

"Yo, Tess. Can we get a round?" Kirian says with Jamie under his arm.

Logan's friend, Karden, comes back to take his seat. His shrewd gaze bounces between us before he picks up his menu.

"Thanks for the shot, Logan."

"My pleasure, Tess."

For the next two hours, I schlep drinks as the band warms up and plays their first set; the crowd filling in with new arrivals. Dawn shows up for work at eight to man the other end of the bar, while her fiancé, Corey, works security. Friday nights with Puppy Love playing are always good tip nights, but the crowd can get a little rowdy. Although at nine o'clock, the night is still too young for a brawl. Those usually happen around closing time.

My two hotties have had their dinners and are talking animatedly about tales from their past. Neither seems drunk, although both have had a couple of beers each, and no matter where I move around the bar, I find Logan's eyes on me.

I've also noticed how he and Karden have waved off every woman who has had the guts to come up and ask them to dance. That shouldn't make me happy, but it does.

"Can I get you anything else?" I ask when the band takes their first break.

"How about your phone number?" Logan says.

I bat my eyelashes. "Awww, I bet you ask that of all the girls."

"I really don't. What time do you get off?"

"Why? Do you think I'm going home with you?"

He sighs, clearly exasperated by me. "No, but I'd like to know you made it home safely."

"That's sweet, but I've made it home safely for the last four years, so I think I can manage another night."

"Yeah, but I didn't know you for the last four years. If I had, I would've been checking in on you."

"Is he always so bossy?" I direct my question to Karden, who shakes his head.

"I've never seen him be possessive of anyone or anything—ever."

Logan smiles. "You know you're special, don't you, Tess?"

I roll my eyes. "Oh, I bet I am."

He reaches across the bar but doesn't touch me, and while I don't give him my hand, I do give him my attention. "Don't tell me you didn't feel that shot of electricity skitter up your spine the moment our eyes met. I know you did, just like it did for me. Let me take you out tomorrow."

I shake my head. "I'm working tomorrow."

"Here?"

"No, at my other job." I don't know why, but I decline to mention I'll be at the VKC tomorrow. Will he be there? Probably not, considering he's not a K9 trainer, but I'm betting Karden will.

"How about tomorrow night?" He presses. "I'm flying out on Monday, so it has to be tomorrow or Sunday at the latest."

Scoffing, I take a step back from him. "Oh, I get it. You're in town for two nights and in a rush to get me into bed?"

His voice drops into a growl. "I'm not trying to get you in the bed, Tess. I'm asking you out on a date. Preferably to a place where we can talk and hear each other speak. And yes, while I might be leaving on Monday for Thanksgiving, I'm coming back."

He glances at Karden who says nothing, his eyes locked on something or someone or maybe nothing in the distance. It's obvious he's trying to zone out this conversation, refusing to be a part of it. "I'm not going to let this go. So you might as well give me your number."

Arching my brow, I cross my arms over my chest—admittedly framing my full breasts for his perusal. Still... I'm not going to make it easy on him. "If you're coming back to town, I'll give you my number next time."

Logan considers me for a moment, his gaze taking in every inch of me, and nods. "That's fair. Don't get married while I'm gone."

I laugh. He has no idea how appropriate that comment is. "I make no promises."

Both he and Karden stand. He pulls his wallet out

from his back pocket and throws two hundred dollar bills down on the bar.

My jaw drops. "Your tab is eighty bucks—tops."

"Anything left is for you, babe. I'll be back after the holidays."

Dumbfounded, I watch them walk out of the bar and am startled back into reality when Kirian once again calls my name. I sigh and nod in his direction. "Coming right up."

It's an early morning as I load up my baked goods, samples, table displays, and taste tester—Brit the Boxer—and drive ten miles east of Spring City to the Veteran K9 Center. To date, my doggie treats business—Tess's Treats—has been a hobby, as well as a labor of love, considering Brit has more food allergies than my pocketbook can afford.

Specifically corn, wheat, and poultry.

She can't eat some of my treats, but I've found there are plenty of dogs who benefit from carefully curated, human-grade food and treats—and their parents will pay to keep them healthy. Right now I have five clients who pay me to deliver fresh food every week, which means I spend Sundays meal prepping for dogs.

If only I could make it a full-time business.

Jamie is the one who invited me to this fundraiser at

the Veteran K9 Center; otherwise I wouldn't have had a clue it was going on. This is my big shot to get the word out there and pick up a few new local clients, or at least meet other vendors and create a network.

I follow a line of cars and trucks to the south of three big metal buildings and stop as a petite blonde woman approaches my window. "Are you here to set up?"

Nodding, I show her the receipt on my phone. I had to pay one hundred dollars to rent my space for the day, but it all goes to charity, so I figure it's a tax write-off.

"Great. I'm Janey, owner of the Veteran K9 Center."

"It's nice to meet you," I say with genuine enthusiasm. I think it's great a woman owns and operates this.

She flashes me a warm smile. "It's nice to meet you, too. I'm excited to see your products."

"I can't wait to show them to you."

Brit sits up and pushes her face into the tiny space between the back of my seat and the open window.

"Who is this?" Janey chuckles, but I notice she keeps her hands to herself. As a dog trainer with her own dog at her feet, she's got to be smarter than ninety percent of the random people who run up to Brit without an invitation.

"This is Brit."

"So sweet. I love her brindle coloring. How old?"

"She's a little over three."

"Well, I look forward to a more personal greeting later when Macha and I aren't on duty." Pointing to where all the cars have parked, she continues. "You are in vendor spot eight. Park with everyone else and if you need help lugging your stuff from your car to your spot, just grab one of the guys. I'll come around to check on you soon."

"Okay." I roll up my window and follow the cars, stopping where a guy wearing a "volunteer" T-shirt tells me to park. I have a wagon to help me cart my totes of goodies, but I can't carry my two folding tables without making a second trip. Luckily, there are a number of people willing to give me a helping hand.

Of course, this would all be a lot easier if my mom had been home this morning like she was supposed to be. Just another mark in the unreliable column.

Not that I'm counting. I stopped keeping tally when I was fourteen.

Even though it's late November in Colorado, it's a mild day and set to be nearly fifty degrees with little to no wind, so it takes no time to warm up from the exertion of setting up my booth. They configured the tent like a farmer's market, except this is one hundred percent canine-focused.

It's also a party, considering Puppy Love will play this afternoon while a giant BBQ rages into the early evening. After I pack up my stuff, I plan to hang out with Jamie while her husband plays.

Brit is super chill and lays patiently on her cot behind the tables as I do my thing. Before I know it, most of the vendors have set up their wares and are walking around, checking out what the rest of us have to offer.

"These look amazing," an older woman coos, her eyes raking over the pumpkin cookies with icing I made last week.

Chuckling, I nod. "Even though I use human-grade ingredients, I wouldn't recommend them."

She joins me in a laugh. "My Golden is with my husband at our booth. We make pet-safe soaps and salves for irritated skin and chapped paw pads, noses, et cetera. We also have a CBD line we're rolling out soon. Can I buy some cookies?"

"Sure!" I say a little too enthusiastically and open up a brown paper sleeve, sliding in a couple of cookies while completely unaware of our audience.

"Tess's Tasty Treats. Human-grade yummies for your furbaby's tummy," a male voice says smoothly. "And look at that; there's a phone number."

I bring my eyes up to find Logan standing there with my business card between his fingers, a wry grin spreading his perfect lips. He looks even better than he did last night in a pair of fitted jeans, a tight T-shirt over his muscular chest, and a loose flannel hanging over that. He's wearing a baseball cap with the VKC logo on it, which layers an incognito mountain man charm over his movie star good looks.

"You?" I gasp.

"And you," he responds, tilting his head toward the woman waiting with a ten-dollar bill in her hand.

"Oh, sorry." I hand her the bag and take the ten, thanking her for her business. "I'll come by to see your stuff soon."

Her eyes go to Logan, and she gives me a knowing wink. "See you later, dear."

Logan leans over my table to look at Brit. "Is that your Boxer?"

"It is."

"Must be fate. Can I pet her?"

I tilt my head to the side and nod slowly. "You can pet her."

He comes around my table and kneels down, cupping her face in his large hands. Brit instantly eats up the attention, sitting up and stretching her neck into his touch. Before I can stop her, she's climbing his chest, putting her paws on top of his shoulders.

She's such a baby.

"She's beautiful. How long have you had her?"

"Three years." I watch him lovingly caress her coat and a tinge of jealousy runs through me. I'd be lying if I didn't admit to fantasizing about him lovingly running his hands over me when I went to bed. Yeah, I definitely got off to thoughts of my sexy stranger before I fell asleep last night. "Why'd you say it was fate?"

He looks up at me, his eyes trailing over my body before coming up to my face. "I've always wanted a Boxer and plan to get one when I move to town."

"You're moving here?"

Nodding, he lets Brit go and stands, showing me exactly how tall and broad he is. Last night he was on a stool, on the other side of the bar top, so I wasn't exactly sure. But now he's only six inches away—close enough to touch—and I feel the full weight of his honed power. "In January. I have to out-process from the Army and get through the holidays, but then I'm here full time."

"I didn't realize you were in the military," I say.

He raises his eyebrow in challenge. "How could you? We haven't gone on our date yet. You know... the one where we learn all about each other."

I blush and roll my eyes. "Yeah, yeah."

"Now that I know what you're doing today, how about dinner tonight?"

"You really aren't going to give up, are you?"

"I'm really not." He shakes his head.

"Good." I smile, my eyes hitting the treats on my table. As a bartender, I'm used to all kinds of flirting and have heard a variety of come-ons ranging from subdued to downright rude. I know how to blow guys off where egos aren't bruised, tips aren't affected, and my safety isn't at risk, but Logan's flirting is different—a perfect combination of direct and casual.

Or maybe I'm so attracted to him that I don't mind his determination.

He says nothing, but when I look up, I find his green eyes on me and a coy smile on his face. "So, Tess. Dinner?"

"I was going to hang out after the vendor fair to watch the band and eat BBQ."

"Am I invited?"

"Could I keep you away?" I tease.

"If you really didn't want me, I'd leave you alone. But I know you want me *almost* as much as I want you."

"There goes that cockiness again."

"Not cocky, babe. Confident."

VETERAN
K9
TEAM
REPORTING
FOR DUTY

Chapter 3
Logan

There's a rumor amongst men that when they met the one they were going to marry, they just knew. Call it a bolt of lightning, Cupid's arrow, Aphrodite's punch in the face—whatever—once I locked eyes with Tess, I knew she was the one for me.

Even if I wasn't moving to Spring City for the Veteran K9 Center or my battle buddies turned into life-long friends, I'd move here for a shot at a lifetime with her.

"There you are." Janey walks up behind me with her Rottweiler, Macha, at her side, her eyes on Tess and her cookies.

Not those cookies.

"Have you met Janey, owner and operator of VKC?" I say casually, sliding up beside Tess as if I'm introducing my new girlfriend to my new business partner.

Neither of which is true... yet.

"Briefly." Tess looks at me with genuine confusion twisting her mouth.

Janey also raises her brow and then turns her attention to the treats. "You're Jamie's friend, right?"

Tess nods and grabs a quart-sized bag of dog treats out of her tote, handing it to Janey. "I brought the center dogs a smorgasbord of samples. I figure you're particular about what you feed them and I would be honored if they tried them."

"Thanks. I'm sure the kids will love them. Can I ask, is this a hobby or something you hope to do full-time?"

"Full time is the dream, although I'm not sure it's feasible." She shrugs. "Someday, though."

Janey smiles, her eyes coming to me, and I'm instantly reminded about her business idea for the new building. Tess could rent space and sell her wares full-time. I could help make that happen—one of her many dreams I've yet to learn but would like to fulfill. "We get questions about fresh, natural, and organic dog food from our clients all the time, so we should talk soon. Maybe after the holidays?"

"She'll be here," I answer for Tess, flashing both women a smile when I realize neither of them find my *Monty Hall's Let's Make A Deal* routine charming.

Tess rolls her eyes. "I would like that, Janey."

"Okay, well, I'll leave you to your customers. See you at the BBQ tonight?" Janey's eyes bounce to me.

"Absolutely." Tess smiles.

"Great." Janey and Macha walk away, greeting and

chatting with vendors along the way. I stand back, dropping to one knee again to pet Brit while Tess talks with new clients.

After they walk away, she looks down at us and smiles. "She likes you."

"Good, because I plan on spending a lot of time with her—" I waggle my brows "—and you. But for now, I should let you take care of business."

"I guess that would be okay."

I pull out my phone and text her. "Now you have my number. If you need a break, or if my girlfriend here needs a walk, text me and I'll come right over."

"And if you get bored and want a place to chill, I suppose me and your new *girlfriend* would like having you." Tess smiles sweetly and waves to the space behind her. "Bring yourself a chair."

I flash her my most charming smile, the one that used to get me out of trouble as a prep school hellraiser, and throw her a wink before walking away from her booth. There are probably twenty to thirty people here, and it will only get crazier as the morning passes.

Walking into the building, I make a B-line to Karden, who is resting his ass against the edge of his desk with Kiki chilling at his feet.

"Why do you look so happy?" He raises his brow.

"Because the woman of my dreams is outside hocking her cookies."

He narrows his eyes. "Somehow that sounds dirty and possibly illegal."

I chuckle. "Tess, the bartender from last night, is here peddling gourmet dog treats and custom food."

"Wow. That's... serendipitous."

"Right?"

Janey walks in with the bag of treats, setting it down on the table. She removes Macha's muzzle, a safety precaution that Karden bitched about last night. Considering there are many untrained dogs in attendance, the team decided they would muzzle their highly trained, military-grade, war machines while walking through the public space—just in case. Meanwhile, none of the civilian dogs are allowed in the building or the training area without a team member escorting them. All vendors signed a form waving VKC liability if their dog gets into a fight with another dog.

Simply put, the problem and solution will be between the two vendors to hash out.

If I'd been involved in the planning of this event, I would have brought in a liability lawyer to protect the business, but as of this moment, I'm still a spectator.

"How's it going out there?" Karden asks.

Janey nods, rubbing Macha's head and pulling out a cookie for her to taste test. Karden grabs one, sniffs it, and then offers it to Kiki who chomps it down eagerly. Both dogs approve of Tess's treats. "So far, so good. All the vendors are happy. The rescue is working on their adoptions, and the silent auction has a pledge of over ten thousand dollars already. We've run several prospective clients through our training program, and we have both county and city K9 representatives here to show their support."

"That's great," I chirp.

She shrugs. "I wish I had the 3D model of the future site ready so we could sell that, too."

"Next time. Maybe in the spring. Instead of annually, this could be a twice a year event, if it's fiscally beneficial," I offer as an idea.

"I guess we'll see when it is all said and done." Janey leans her hips against the wall and smiles at me. "So... Tess. How long has that been going on?"

I chuckle. "Since eight last night."

Janey's jaw drops. "What is it with you guys? Every single one of you jumps in with both feet."

Shrugging, I glance at Karden, who points to himself and shakes his head, wordlessly stating *Not Me*. "When you know, you know."

She rolls her eyes. "Whatever."

"Who, besides me, are you talking about?" I'm trying to think, but as far as I know, everyone but Vale and Kemp are single. According to Karden, Barron has been married and divorced. Meanwhile, he, Saint, and Lincoln have never had a serious relationship. Long-term arrangements, yeah, but nothing approaching an altar or happily ever after.

None of them have been struck stupid like I was last night.

Janey's gaze drifts across the room, and she shrugs. "No one, I guess."

I exchange a glance with Karden, who subtly shakes his head and presses his lips together. There have been rumors about Janey and Saint over the years, mostly from a time before I knew any of them, but no one knows anything for sure. You're likely to get your bell rung if you push Saint for more information, and as a woman, we don't ask Janey.

When she was in the military, she worked hard to present and maintain a professional image.

I guess in some ways she still does.

"Do we have any coffee or hot cocoa or something? I think I'll bring Tess a mug." I glance around at the same time Kemp and Vale walk in with their dogs. Kemp eyes the bag of cookies and grabs a pumpkin-shaped one with icing, sniffing it before taking a bite.

He grimaces. "This is horrible."

Karden and I laugh, while Janey says, "It's for Krieger, dumbass."

Handing his Shepherd the biscuit, he grabs a napkin and wipes his tongue. "Why do they make them so appealing to humans? It's not like the dog cares about presentation."

"Because humans are the ones with the cash, and we are visually stimulated creatures." Vale chuckles, grabbing another one and feeding it to his Husky, Strijker.

"Speaking of visually stimulating things." I waggle my brow.

Janey shakes her head. "There is a gourmet coffee truck outside. Buy her something fancy."

"Good idea." I smack Karden on the shoulder and leave the K9 crew behind to do their thing.

Twenty minutes later, I'm walking up to Tess's table with four drinks. I have no idea what she likes, so I bought a smattering of everything. One fancy s'mores mocha latte, a caramel apple cider, decaf black coffee, and a regular black coffee for me. I figure if she wants something different, I'll get it for her.

There's an attractive, older woman with a salt-and-pepper gentleman standing at the end of her table, almost behind it with an air of familiarity.

Tess's eyes grow wide when I set down the tray of drinks. "Can I tempt you with something hot?"

She blushes and squares her shoulders. I love how she doesn't back down from my flirting, even if she mutes her responses to be nearly innocent. I wonder if that's a byproduct of working as a bartender? No doubt men are up her ass nightly, shooting their shots.

"What are you offering?"

I run through the drinks, thankful she takes the s'mores with enthusiasm, and look up to find the woman smiling at me. She's the spitting image of Tess in fifteen to twenty years. So much so that they are obviously related. Dark, lush, long hair. Light brown, almost gray eyes. Thick, long eyelashes, and centerfold curves. I'm not going to say she has the same plump, kissable lips, considering I don't know if this is a mother or an older sister, but I bet the guy standing next to her has no complaints. "I don't suppose you like black decaf coffee or caramel apple cider?"

"I'll take the cider if you're offering." She smiles.

"Sure thing." I hand her the cup and then look at

Tess, hoping she feels it is necessary to introduce me. When she takes a second too long to stare at me, I tilt my head to encourage her.

She rolls her eyes. "Logan, this is my mother, Tracy, and her man friend, Steve."

"Nice to meet you, Tracy." I shake her hand and then look at her *man friend*—which is an interesting term to use. There's a story there. "Can I interest you in a decaf, Steve?"

The salt-and-pepper man nods and holds his hand out. "Thanks."

I shake his hand and then turn my attention back to Tess as she takes her first sip.

"Mmmm." She lets out a low moan that causes the lower half of my body to tingle. I'd love to coax those sounds out of her often.

"Are you the hot guy getting me out of trouble this morning?" Tracy smiles over her steaming cup of cider.

"Trouble?" I let the *hot guy* comment slide— for now.

"My mom was supposed to be my second pair of hands this morning, but she was otherwise occupied," Tess says with a bit of bite.

"Oh?" I say, a bit confused, but then catch the way Tracy and Steve glance at each other. "Ohhhh. Well, as far as excuses go, it's a pretty good one."

"Don't encourage her," Tess mutters, turning on a bright smile as another customer approaches the table.

"Well—" Tracy grabs Brit's leash and flashes me a big smile "—we are going to take this princess for a walk, cruise the other vendors, and will be back soon. Nice to meet you, Logan."

As they leave, I stand to the side and wait for the customers to clear Tess's table. Once they are gone, she turns to me and shakes her head. "Don't ask."

"Oh, but I have to know," I say with a teasing lilt.

She chuckles. "My mom had me when she was young, and while I love her very much, she's not the most reliable person in my life. We kind of raised each other."

"Are you an only child?" I can't help myself and reach out to brush a piece of her hair that's fallen loose from her braid out of her face.

"I am. Are you?"

"No, but I'm definitely the black sheep of my family."

"I don't believe that. You're too handsome to be trouble to anyone other than women and their panties."

I take a step closer and finger the length of her braid. "You admit you find me attractive?"

Tess's eyes sparkle, her lips parting in surprise, but she doesn't step back. She doesn't turn away from me. She's bold and fearless—two traits that completely turn me on. "You don't need me to stroke your ego, Logan."

"Maybe not, but that doesn't mean I wouldn't enjoy it." My eyes shift to the side, and I take a reluctant step back so Tess can turn her attention to another customer.

A few minutes later, Karden walks through with Kiki muzzled and on her leash, a camping chair in his hand. "Figured you could use a seat."

"Thanks."

He nods his head to Tess in greeting and then fingers

a bag of treats. "The dogs approve. Thanks for the sample pack."

Her smile is wide. "You're welcome. I'm thrilled they like them."

"Are you hanging out with us after the vendor fair?"

"Yes." She nods enthusiastically.

Karden gives me a meaningful look before walking away. "I guess I'll be seeing you both later."

"Later, man." I set up the chair but don't take a seat. "Can I get you something to eat?"

Tess chuckles. "You don't have to take care of me, Logan."

"Maybe I want to take care of you."

"Yeah, right." She sits on a little stool in the corner behind her table that I hadn't noticed. "Sit down and talk to me."

"What do you want to know?" I move my seat closer to hers and sit down.

"Why are you the black sheep of your family?"

"Uh, well, that's an involved story."

"The crowd is thinning out, but maybe you can give me the short version."

I lean back in the chair and blow out my breath. "My family has certain expectations, an image they put out to the world that I chose not to conform to by joining the Army. But honestly, I was a disappointment long before that."

"Do you hope to one day win their approval?" Tess arches her brow and takes a sip of her drink, which by now is lukewarm.

"Not really. I'm happy with the man I've become." I grab her hand, inspecting the tattoos on her forearm. Flowers and paw prints in bright colors trail up her arms, wrap around her shoulder, and dance across her chest, which is covered today by a high neck Henley stretched taut over her breasts. "Don't get me wrong, I'm not estranged from them. We talk once or twice a month, but I have no desire to be pulled back into the fold."

"Sounds ominous."

"Definitely something I'd rather discuss over a drink in a dark, quiet location."

Tess wraps her fingers over my forearm in understanding. "Okay."

"Is it just you and your mom?"

She nods. "And Brit living in a two bedroom, two bath townhouse. Neither of us can afford to move out, and considering we're more like roommates, it works out fine."

"What about Steve?" I raise my brow.

Tess shrugs. "Steve is new, so we will see how long he lasts, but he seems like a nice enough guy."

The vendors next to us pack up their tables, and I check my watch. "It's thirteen hundred hours. Looks like the vendor's fair part of the day is over. How'd you do?"

"I'm pretty sure I broke even. Sold out of my treat bags, made a couple of new clients, and paid for all my ingredients and the table fee, with maybe a little left over."

"That's fantastic. Can I help you pack up and carry

things to your car?" I glance around, wondering where Brit and Tracy got off to.

"That'd be nice, thank you."

After packing her totes and tables in her older Xterra, we walk around to the other side of the three buildings where they erected a makeshift stage and the band Puppy Love sets up their equipment. Brit, Tracy, and Steve are standing with Jamie from last night and a dog, who I assume is her Husky, Nanook.

"There you are," Tess says, giving Jamie a quick hug.

"Hey!" Jamie seems a bit surprised and wraps her arms around Tess. Her eyes shoot to me and then she nods in my direction. "Hello."

I offer her my hand, my shoulder brushing Tess's because we are standing so close. "We didn't get introduced last night. I'm Logan."

"Nice to meet you." Jamie worries her bottom lip between her teeth, her eyes bouncing between me and Tess. "Uh, girl, there's something I should remind you about."

"What's that?" Tess takes Brit's leash from Tracy, and it's only then that I notice both women are tossing me uncomfortable glances.

"Dave is here."

"Dave?" I ask. "Who is Dave?"

"Shit," Tess mutters. "What the hell is he doing here?"

"He sponsored the band. Remember?"

I glance around and zero in on a decent-looking guy

staring down at us from the stage, the intensity in his gaze answering my question. "Is that Dave?"

Tess looks at me and then follows my eyes up to the stage. "Shit, shit, shit."

Well, fuck me.

That can't be good.

And still, no one has answered my question.

Who the fuck is Dave?

VETERAN
K9
TEAM
REPORTING
FOR DUTY

Chapter 4
Tess

Fuck my life.

I completely forgot my ex-fiancé sponsored Puppy Love for this gig. As a charity event, Dave said it was a tax write-off. Considering he has more money than brains, heart, or morals, he said yes months ago without bringing it up again.

Honestly, I think he likes being the guy hosting the party, even when he doesn't understand what the celebration is for.

"Who is this guy, Tess?" Logan says so low, I'm the only one to hear him.

"That's another long story," I say under my breath as Dave jumps off the front of the stage, his stride in our direction strong and sure.

It's been a month since I caught him cock deep in some chick dressed as a slutty nurse at the bar's Halloween party.

Right there in the ladies' room of the Last Stand.

Fucking classy.

"Give me the Cliffs notes," Logan says calmly.

"He's my lying, cheating, self-absorbed, douchebag ex…"

That's all I get out before Dave stops in front of us, his gaze swinging from me to Logan and back again. "I was hoping you'd be here today."

"And I completely forgot you existed," I respond coolly.

He smiles, his eyes sliding to Logan, his hand shooting out in greeting. "I'm Dave. Tess's fiancé."

"Ex-fiancé," I remind him.

"Ex." He nods, his mouth twisting as if I've told a joke. "We're on a break, so whatever this is—" he says to Logan, motioning between us with a casual wave of his fingers "—I'll allow. As long as you realize that your time with her is temporary."

"You are such a dick," I seethe. "We are never getting back together."

Dave's smile gets even wider. "Of course we are, sweetheart. Preferably before Christmas, so you can go skiing with me in B.C. You don't want to miss that, do you?"

"Fuck you."

Logan slides his hand into mine and squeezes my fingers. "Come on, babe. We've got that thing to get to."

He pulls me gently, giving me ample opportunity to shrug off the lifeline he's giving me.

But I don't.

And I won't.

Because I can't.

"Come on, Brit." I give a slight tug of her leash and follow Logan, his grip on my hand growing tighter with every step we take. He doesn't say a word to me, walking right up to Janey and Kemp with their dogs.

"You got an office we can dip into for ten minutes?"

Janey glances down at Brit. "Yeah, you can use the conference room, but announce to the guys you have a civilian dog with you."

"Roger." Logan nods and pulls me into the training facility—the one we're not supposed to bring our animals into without an escort.

We don't have time to announce ourselves before Karden and Kiki walk out of a cluster of small offices to the right. Logan looks at him and then points to the left. "We're going in here for a few minutes, and then I need to talk to you."

Karden's brow furrows. "Uh, okay."

Logan lets go of my fingers and slides his hand to the small of my back, ushering me through the door that he closes behind him. I let Brit's leash fall from my hand before slumping into a chair. She's attuned to my moods, and instantly puts her head in my lap to let me stroke her soft muzzle.

"Are you okay?" Logan says calmly—too calmly. Up until this moment, he's been an absolute charmer, but something tells me he's not the one to piss off or double-cross. I'm not sure if I find that unbelievably sexy or scary.

Maybe a bit of both.

"I'm sorry about that."

He sits in the chair in front of me and shakes his head. "You have nothing to apologize for. Last night I didn't ask about a boyfriend, fiancé, or husband because I figured if you had one, you'd have told me to pound sand. That guy is an obvious assclown who, for some reason, thinks he owns you."

"Assclown?" I giggle. "That's a good one. I like it."

"You're welcome to use it." Logan leans forward in his chair, strokes Brit's neck, and then takes my hand in his. "Look, Tess. I pulled you in here for two reasons. One, I figured you needed an escape, and two, I need to know if there is any truth to his claim. Are you only on a break?"

"No." I shake my head. There is so much more to say, but at the same time, I do not want to unload on Logan. Doing so would certainly send him running for the hills. We might have just met, but he wasn't wrong when he said there was an instant connection last night that feels even stronger today. I've never felt like that with a guy before, and I'm not even sure what *that* is.

"Good. Because I have to be straight with you. I'm not a temporary kind of guy, and I don't covet other people's things, whether it be property or relationships. I'm also not going to be chased away by some guy just because he lays claim to you."

I sigh. "He cheated on me—many, many times. But honestly, catching him in the act was the ammunition I needed to end it with him. Yes, we were *engaged*, but it wasn't real. At least not in my eyes."

I shake my head, unable to stop the word vomit spewing out of me. "Dave is an entitled rich kid who is used to getting what he wants. He thinks money solves every problem, especially when he is the problem. Dating him was fine, but..."

Embarrassed about what I'm about to say, I cast my eyes down to the smooth, reddish-brown concrete floor. "He took me to nice places and on expensive vacations that I never would've been able to go on otherwise. I know it's wrong, but I was always clear about my feelings. We were having fun. That's it. When he proposed, he didn't let me say yes or no. He just slid the ring on my finger and told me to wear it until I got used to it."

I shrug. "I don't know why I wore the ring for as long as I did. I guess I liked it on my finger."

"Did you love him?" he asks softly.

"No. He knew that, but he didn't care." Pressing my lips together, I shake my head. "There are all kinds of jerks out there, but the ones with money are the worst."

Logan lets go of my hand and sits back, saying nothing.

I know he's disgusted by me, and I don't blame him. I'm quickly turning into my mother, despite my best attempts to be nothing like her. She never got over my dad—the only man I think she remotely loved. He lived his life on his terms, despite having a kid in Spring City.

Truth be told, they both did.

Throughout my childhood, they dated other people, and while he sired many kids across the country—three in total that I know of—we only acted like a family for the few weeks he rolled into town. He never married, but he put all of his kids on his military benefits, so at least I had health care.

My father loved hard, but couldn't commit. He died when I was twelve in a freak helicopter accident while training in Arizona. It was our portion of his insurance that paid for the townhouse we live in now.

My mother has also had many love affairs spanning months to years, but she never committed either. She let men come into our lives—pamper us, take us on family vacations, even pay our bills from time to time—but she never let them move in with us, even if she spent most nights of the week in their beds, leaving me to fend for myself, home alone.

She never accepted their marriage proposals either—of which there were many.

She never let herself fall in love again.

Like mother, like daughter.

Looking up, I find Logan's green gaze on me. I can't read him, can't tell what he's thinking, but I guess he's thinking, *I didn't sign up for this shit.*

I sigh and push to my feet. "It's been a long day, so Brit and I are going home. It was nice meeting you, Logan."

He quickly stands and grabs my hand before I can step away, pulling me flush against his amazingly hard and chiseled body. Before I know it, his hand is in my hair and he's cupping my head as he lowers his lips to mine.

It's a simple kiss, sweet and unassuming, but it does the trick and turns me into a pile of goo. I sag into his embrace, my lips parting in invitation. One slip of his tongue into my mouth and I'm lost, ready to give him whatever he wants.

"What was that for?" I whisper when he pulls back a fraction of an inch and peers down at me with those mesmerizing green eyes.

"If there's no future with him, then I hope you'll consider a future with me."

"You just met me."

"When you know, you know." He shrugs. "I was certain about you the moment I laid eyes on you, and I'm hoping you feel something for me, too. If not before our kiss, certainly afterward."

"That kiss has me feeling something alright—" I waggle my brows "—but what are you asking me?"

Logan grins and swipes his thumb over my bottom lip. "For a chance to get to know each other."

"I'd like that."

There's a knock at the door, but Logan doesn't release his hold on me. "Yeah?"

The door cracks open, and Janey sticks her head in. "Can I come in?"

"Sure." Logan takes a step back, but wraps his fingers through the belt loop of my jeans, holding me next to him. Brit makes a move to greet the trainer, who is without her Rottweiler at the moment.

"Jamie said Dave Mansfeld is your ex. Are we going to have a problem?" Janey looks from me to Logan and then back to me as she pets Brit's head.

"No." I flash her a smile that doesn't quite reach my

eyes.

"If I could, I'd ask him to leave, but he paid for the next four hours of entertainment." she says apologetically.

Logan shakes his head. "It's fine. My girl can handle herself, and if he oversteps her boundaries, I'll be there."

"Okay, well, we're getting ready to announce the silent auction winners and then the BBQ and band will start. Are you staying?"

Logan looks at me and whispers, "I got you."

I nod. "It sounds like we're staying."

"Good. Me and the K9 guys are hanging out on the left side of the stage, if you want to chill with us." Janey bends down and gives Brit another head scratch. "She seems like she'll be good with our dogs, but we'll introduce them one at a time, just in case."

She walks out, and Logan leans forward, pressing another kiss to my lips. "Sorry, but now that I've had a taste, I'm going to want to do that a lot."

"Does that go for every other taste we take as we get to know each other?" I arch my brow, glad we're back to light and flirty. This is where I'm comfortable, and things got too serious there for a second.

"Absolutely." His eyes travel slowly over my body, causing a tingle to skitter down my spine and settle in my pussy. Damn, the reactions I've had to this man from the moment our eyes met last night are surreal.

We walk together towards the left side of the stage, introducing Brit to Kiki, Macha, Strijker, Sookie, and Krieger.

Karden and Kemp nod their heads. "Brit is well trained for a Boxer her age. Very chill."

"Yeah, I took her to training when she was a puppy because I wanted her to go wherever I went."

"Which trainer?"

"Gary off of Janitell and the freeway."

"Yeah, we've heard of him. Good guy?"

"I thought so." I look up to see my mom and Steve walking toward us as Janey and Macha take the stage.

Kemp barks a strangled noise and says, "Shit. I'm supposed to be up there with her. Excuse me."

My mom smiles at Logan. "Everything okay?"

I look around, noting Dave on the other side of the stage with a couple of his buddies. He's watching me with a smirk on his lips, as if this is a game we like to play —some kind of sick and twisted foreplay I never signed up for.

God, I really ha... dislike him. Hate is a strong word, so I try to never use it, but it's on the tip of my tongue just the same.

I slyly flash him the middle finger and turn to answer my mom. "Yeah, everything's fine."

She slides up to my side opposite Logan and whispers in my ear. "I like this guy. Why haven't you told me about him?"

"Because I literally met him last night."

"Oh? With the chemistry between the two of you, I would've thought you'd known each other for a lot longer."

I glance at Logan who is staring at Janey on the stage.

He waggles his brow, letting me know that he's paying attention, even though he's not looking at us.

Janey is at the microphone with Kemp by her side. "Hey everyone. My name is Janey LaVey, and I am the owner of the Veteran K9 Center. With me is Michael Kemp, Chief Operations Officer—or lead dude in charge, if you will. We're not really formal enough for CEO and COO titles, even if that's what the business license says."

Logan and Karden chuckle and I get the team/family vibe they have together, the Army or military bond men and women have that the rest of us can't quite comprehend.

"We want to thank everybody for being here today. This is our first Paws for a Cause fundraiser, and it has been a wonderful success. Valley Heights had multiple dogs adopted today, and now we're going to talk about why we're raising money. The VKC has been open for almost three years, and for anybody who didn't know, it was originally opened to provide military members a safe place to kennel and train their dogs, specifically when they get pulled away from home on training exercises, schools, and of course, deployments. For the last year, we've been researching the possibility of training and placing PTSD support animals with qualified military veterans, and today is step one in realizing that dream. It costs roughly twenty thousand dollars and over a year to train a support animal, and we recently got several of our canine handlers certified to do just that. Plus, we'll be getting our first few puppies next month."

"Most importantly, there's no cost to the veterans

who qualify for and receive a support animal, which is why all the donations accumulated today are so very important to our goal," Kemp adds.

"Right." Janey looks in our direction. "To the left of the stage are the K9 handlers and team members who are working to make this and bigger things happen soon. If you have questions about the program or how you can help, just find one of us wearing a VKC T-shirt or hat. Again, thank you for your donations and support. Now, I'll turn the microphone over to Cherise and Mari as they announce the silent auction winners."

"I wonder what bigger things are happening soon?" I say to no one in particular.

Logan slides his hand into mine and squeezes my fingers gently. "If you really want to know, I'll tell you later. I think you'll be excited about it."

I look at him, my brow furrowed, and realize that I haven't asked him why he's in town this weekend. "You know, I assumed you knew these guys from the military, but it never dawned on me to ask why you're here today."

"Babe, we have so much to learn about each other. Yes, some of us served together, but I'm investing in the future of this business. And that is one reason I'm moving to town."

"What's the other reason?"

He looks at me and flashes me the same charming smile he gave me last night. "Do you really need to ask?"

I roll my eyes. "You are a lot, you know that?"

"Yeah, but you like it."

VETERAN
K9
TEAM
REPORTING
FOR DUTY

Chapter 5
Logan

We set up a couple of chairs with the guys, a cooler of drinks between us and them. The BBQ is fantastic—served by a food truck with some of the best brisket I've ever had.

The four Bs—BBQ, beer, band, and beautiful babe—make for a perfect afternoon.

But now the sun is dipping in the west and the temperature has dropped at least ten degrees in a matter of minutes.

Puppy Love will play for another hour, and I'm keenly aware that Dave has been watching us with a feigned casual eye the entire time from the other side of the stage. He doesn't bother me personally. I'm used to someone coveting what is mine, but his creepy stare makes me worry about her.

Will he become unhinged if he doesn't get his way?

How can I protect her when I'm not here?

His entitled and spoiled behavior tainted her opinion

of people with money, so I'm not sure how I'm going to handle that. I don't know him or his family, but I'd be surprised if they have more money or affluence than mine.

Not that it matters. I stopped being interested in buying friends or fame when I was a teenager—hence why I joined the Army.

Still. Someday Tess will meet my family. Will they turn her off of a future with me?

"It's getting cold. Did you bring a jacket?" Tess leans into me, so I can hear her over the band.

"Yeah, but it's in the car."

"Do you want to get out of here?" She arches her eyebrow.

I take her hand in mine and bring it to my lips. "What did you have in mind, babe?"

"Well, I think my mom is staying the night with Steve again. Do you want to watch a movie?"

I want to.

Goddamn, I want to.

But I've been aggressively pursuing her from the moment I laid eyes on her, and I don't want her to think this is a one-and-done thing for me. I know she's mine, but now that I've learned about Dave, I need to distance myself from that asshole in her head.

Plus, until I tell her the whole truth about who I am and my family, I shouldn't cross any lines that she'd consider a betrayal.

"Are you inviting me over to your house?"

She shrugs. "I need to get Brit home, and honestly,

I've been up since six after closing down the bar last night at two. I would love nothing more than to take a shower, slip into my PJs, and relax for a little while."

"If you're tired, why don't we call it a night?"

"I thought you wanted to take me out?"

"I do, but we don't have to rush anything, Tess. I'm leaving town on Monday, and I'll be gone through the new year, but then I'm back. Permanently. We have all the time in the world to get to know each other."

She smiles softly and looks down at my hand on her knee. I haven't been able to stop myself from touching her, even in the most innocent way. "What are you doing tomorrow, Logan?"

"Whatever you want to do, babe."

"Well, I'm actually making and delivering dog food for most of the day, but if you want to hang out with me while I do it, I'd love for you to keep me company."

"It's a date." I stand up and pull her to her feet. "Let me walk you to your car."

The next morning, I pull up to the address Tess texted me with two breakfast burritos, a box of donuts, and two coffees. After walking her to her SUV, I leaned down to take what was supposed to be a simple goodnight kiss and ended up making out with her for a solid ten minutes—until I was so achingly hard that I had to take a lap around the buildings before I could walk comfortably and rejoin the guys.

I've been thinking about that kiss all night and again this morning as I jerked off in the shower.

She's so beautiful—everything about this woman turns me on. But it's more than her looks. It's her flirty confidence that I find so sexy, as well as her drive and passion, both of which are intoxicating.

"Hey." She opens the door with a smile. "I wasn't sure you'd make it."

"Why is that?" I hand her the donut box and then lean forward to kiss her cheek before following her into the townhouse.

"I put some of my best moves on you last night and you still sent me home by myself." She shrugs and leads me into the kitchen. "I figured after the whole Dave thing, maybe you weren't interested."

I put our drinks and burritos down next to the donut box and then slide my hands around her waist, pulling her flush against my body. "Nothing could be further from the truth, but I will admit, after meeting Dave, I figured I should tone it down. The last thing I want is for you to put me in the same category as him."

"You're confident, not cocky. Remember?" She smiles up at me.

I nod. "That's true. I'm glad you recognize the difference."

"I saw it Friday night, but I couldn't make it easy on you."

"You can make me work for it." I kiss the tip of her nose. "I don't mind."

"I was thinking about you this morning." She pulls out of my embrace and eyes the coffee, handing me the one that is plain black.

"Yeah, I was thinking about you, too." I take my coffee, slipping her a sly wink.

Her eyes trail down my body, sending blood straight to my cock, and flashes me a knowing grin. "My thoughts were a bit more PG."

"Probably." I help myself in her kitchen, opening cupboards and pulling down two plates.

Tess pulls out two stools, and we sit down at the breakfast bar, unwrapping our breakfast burritos as if we've done this a dozen times. "They weren't one hundred percent PG, but that's a discussion for later."

I stop with the burrito midway to my mouth and glance at her, a devilish smirk on her lips. "Are you teasing me?"

"Maybe a little."

"I like it."

She chuckles and rolls her eyes as I take a big bite of my meal.

"What does *investing in the business* look like? I didn't think soldiers made a ton of money."

I shrug. "Base pay is a little more than minimum wage if we worked forty-hour weeks, which, of course, we don't. But there are other incentives, like housing allowance, education, and medical benefits. And if you do twenty years, there's retirement to look forward to."

"But you aren't doing twenty?" She whispers.

"No. Six was enough for me." I leave it at that, skirting the topic of money or my reasons for leaving. I don't want to outright lie, but I don't want it to be a thing between us, either, at least not until I move to town and we can face any concerns she has together.

"So what does your investment look like? Are you going to work at VKC? Sponsor a dog? Build kennels?"

"Uh—" I hedge "—I have an inheritance left to me by my great-grandfather. Now that I've turned twenty-five, I have to go to Cali to meet with the lawyers and sign some paperwork. After Christmas, I'll move here and invest in the next phase of the center to include retail spaces... say, for a small business owner who makes and sells gourmet dog treats."

"Oh." She shakes her head. "I'm nowhere near able to afford a retail space."

"Maybe not today, but by the time we're ready, who knows?"

Tess bites her lip and glances around her kitchen, an air of wistfulness in her expression. "It's nice your great-grandfather put something aside for you."

I shrug, desperate to change the subject. I've been downplaying my familial connections and bank account since I entered the military six years ago, and while I'm not ashamed of my family, I spent the first eighteen years of my life being sucked up to because of my last name, and not because of who I am as a person.

I really want Tess to like me as a person.

"Have you ever been to Southern California?"

She nods, swallowing her bite of burrito. "One of my mom's boyfriends took us to Disneyland when I was like eight or nine. And then another time we went to Hollywood and Universal Studios, and those kinds of places when I was fifteen. That was kind of creepy."

"Why is that?"

"I developed young, so the amount of men hitting on me and my mother simultaneously was gross."

"There are creeps everywhere, but Hollywood has a special brand of sycophant, one that likes to use the guise of discovering raw talent to perpetuate their lecherous ways. Maybe someday you'll come to California with me and I'll show you a different side of So Cal."

She smiles and glances down at my nearly empty plate. "That would be cool. Are you ready to make dog food?"

I laugh. "That is a question I never thought I would be asked."

She chuckles. "I'm glad I can provide you with new experiences."

We put our dishes into the dishwasher, and then Tess takes considerable time clearing the space. I sit on the floor with Brit, staying out of her way while bonding with the easygoing Boxer.

For the next couple hours, I watch her prep ingredients, portion out servings, and vacuum seal seven days' worth of food for her clients—old and new. "This is quite the operation you've got going here."

"Yeah, I don't know what I'm going to do when I outgrow this space. I've talked to Max about using the bar's kitchen, but that means I have to change my days and hours. But at least there's an option there."

I store that tidbit of information in my brain for later. I have to admit, I never thought watching somebody make dog food would be inspirational. She certainly cares about what she's creating, labeling each bag with ingredients and potential allergens. The way she sources her raw meat is impressive, too. This is not just some hobby, but a passion to take care of her—and other people's—furbabies, as she calls them.

I worry about her liabilities, though, especially if she grows her business. She has nothing legally protecting her in case a dog has an adverse reaction to her treats. That is something I will rectify once I move into town.

"Now what?" I dry my hands on the towel she offers me after washing and rinsing the last bowl.

"Now we deliver the food. Are you up for a joyride?"

"Definitely. Maybe you can give me a tour of the neighborhoods while we're at it."

"I can do that. I'll even show you my favorite house of all time."

"That would be good because I'm going to need to look for a place to live, and I need to know which neighborhoods are the right ones to move into." And of course, buying a house Tess likes in a neighborhood she eventually wants to live in just makes good financial sense.

I know I'm getting ahead of myself, but I feel our connection in my bones.

Does she?

We climb into her Xterra, with Brit taking a seat in

the back, and spend the next two hours driving. "If you could live anywhere in or around Spring City, which neighborhood would you pick?" I ask casually.

"Is money a factor?"

I shake my head. "Not really."

She hums, deep in thought for a minute. "It depends on what I had going on in my life. If I need to be in town near a job, I'd probably move to Peregrine or maybe down south near Castilla Mountain. There are big beautiful houses in good school districts in those neighborhoods, but most of them don't have land to offer. There's Vanguard Estates, which is a newer, gated community where at least half of the Rocky Mountain Rangers football team lives in their mini-mansions on one-acre lots, but I don't think I'd like living there. Starlite Park is an established community with one- to five-acre lots—they even zoned some as horse properties. Northeast, near the VKC, people have five- to ten-acre hobby farms that might be fun for kids."

"Do you want kids?" I look at her through a different lens and picture her five years from now with a toddler on her lap resting their dark hair against her swollen belly.

Holy shit, I never have thoughts like this. Yet with Tess, they feel natural.

"I do. At least two, but maybe three or four. You?" She glances over at me after negotiating a left turn into a nice neighborhood.

"Yeah. Someday." I nod, more certain now than I ever have been. Children have always been a mystery to me, mostly because I'm the baby of the family and spent most of my life raised by nannies or living away from home amidst other prep school kids—out of sight, out of mind.

And my mother couldn't understand how joining the Army and living in the barracks with a dozen other guys felt so natural to me.

She parks in front of a large house with a faux brick facade accenting the doorway. "Let me take these up, and then I'll drive you through the Gold Rush Hills Estates. They are beautiful houses overlooking the city."

While she runs up to the house, I jot a note of the neighborhoods she's listed, letting the real estate agent Karden hooked me up with know I want something with a couple of acres that are zoned for animals and five or more bedrooms. She'll send me listings to look at after the holiday, and if things continue to go well, I'll ask Tess to do me a favor by touring the houses with the realtor and FaceTiming me during their walk-throughs.

I'll let her pick our future home, even if she doesn't know that's what she's doing.

Karden laughed at me last night when I told him my plan. He said it was ridiculous to jump headfirst into a relationship with a woman who doesn't know I'm working toward forever with her.

My response: if you aren't working toward forever, what are you doing?

Passing time was his answer, and I guess he's right. Until now, I've been passing time, but with Tess, I know this is more.

Maybe I'm crazy, but I'm trusting my gut and my gut tells me she's the one.

Tess jogs back to her SUV with a big smile on her face. "They have a very sweet English Bulldog who had a medley of digestive problems before she started eating my food."

"It makes you happy to help people and their furbabies."

She nods, the smile on her face growing wider. "It really does."

"How about we grab some dinner?"

"Actually, I was thinking we would order takeout and watch the game. The Rangers are playing Atlanta tonight."

"You like football?"

Tess shrugs. "I like our home team, and if I can catch a game, I will. Do you like football?"

"Yes, but I don't schedule my day around it."

"Here's a million-dollar question for you. Who is your team?" Tess raises her brow in challenge, a sassy smirk spreading her lips.

"I guess I better say the Rangers, huh?" I smile back.

"You don't have to, but if you root against my team, I'll hurt you." She winks.

I grab her hand and pull it to my lips, placing a gentle kiss against her fingers. "I would gladly wrestle with you."

"Would you let me win?"

Heat infuses my chest and my eyes trace over her lush curves. "Absolutely."

Giggling, she shakes her head and pulls her hand from mine. "Do you like Thai food?"

"I love it."

She does a happy dance in her seat. "There's a great place a couple of blocks from my house. It's my favorite."

"Let's do it."

We grab the food and head home. After eating, we sit on the couch and watch the first half of the game as the Rangers beat Atlanta. During halftime, I lean against the edge of the couch and pull her between my legs, wrapping my arms loosely around her as she lays her head against my chest. Nuzzling her neck, I whisper in her ear. "This is nice."

"It is. I don't think I've ever truly snuggled before."

"Are guys always in a hurry to get into your pants?" I press a chaste kiss to her temple.

"Yeah. Or maybe I'm always in a hurry to get the deed done. I'm not great with intimacy, and most guys don't care about it, anyway."

"Does it make you uncomfortable?" I kiss her cheek and turn her chin so our eyes meet.

"Intimacy translates to vulnerability in my mind."

I brush a strand of hair back from her cheek and kiss her lips softly. "I'm not asking for anything I'm not willing to give. You do your best to match my energy, and I'll be a happy man. If at any point you decide you aren't feeling what I'm feeling, talk to me about it. Okay?"

Tess smiles and slides her fingers along the shaved sides of my head, ignoring my request. "Do you think you'll grow your hair when you separate from the military?"

"Maybe a little. Why?"

"I wonder what you'll look like."

"Someday I'll show you pictures of me as a teen. I went through a surfer dude phase at one point. Long hair, puka shell necklace, golden tan—the stereotypical So-Cal beach bum image." I lean down and claim her lips in a kiss that I hope will keep her on edge and pining for me over the next six weeks. Our tongues tangle as she adjusts her position on my lap, meeting me with just as much passion and need.

"What time is your flight tomorrow?" She pants when we break for air.

"Eight a.m. out of Denver. Karden says I'll have to leave his place no later than five if I want to make my flight."

"I guess that means you won't be tucking me into bed tonight." Tess juts her bottom lip in feigned disappointment, although it might not be completely fake. She wants me as much as I want her. The chemistry between us is explosive. Everyone sees it—even her mother.

"Not tonight, babe." I glance at my watch, knowing if I don't leave now, I might never leave. "I should head out before we get carried away."

She lets me up and walks me to the door, where I once again pull her into my arms. "I'll be back soon, and we'll talk every day until then. Okay?"

"Okay." She nods and smiles, but her tone is full of doubt. How can she question my sincerity? Has she been fed bullshit throughout her life and cannot accept anything else? Considering I'm holding back some of my truth right now, maybe I shouldn't push it.

"Goodnight." I kiss her softly and pull back, forcing myself to let her go. The coldness from the night air combined with the distance between us chills me to the bone. I walk back to my rental and slide into the driver's seat, cranking the engine and illuminating the house with my headlights as she waves and closes the front door.

My heart pounds in my chest, and I know I can't leave just yet.

It's not enough to have the memory of her body pressed against mine, or the velvety softness of her tongue sliding into my mouth. To survive the next month without her, I need the smell of her arousal infusing my lungs and the taste of her orgasm sliding down my throat.

I turn off the engine and jump out of my car with one more task to complete before I leave—making my woman come.

VETERAN
K9
TEAM
REPORTING
FOR DUTY

Chapter 6
Tess

I close the door and shuffle into the kitchen, an uneasiness settling in my tummy.

"He's a gentleman, Tess," I say out loud to reassure myself. How sad is it that if a guy isn't pawing at me nonstop, I assume he's not interested or he has some big secret to hide?

It's pathetic.

There's a knock on my front door and then Logan is standing in my entryway, shaking his head and flipping the deadbolt into the engaged position. "You should lock your doors, babe."

I smile. "Maybe I was hoping you'd come back?"

Logan approaches me like a man on a mission, pulling me against his body before swinging me up into his arms. "I need one thing from you before I leave."

"What's that, Logan?" I grin.

"You—coming on my lips." He sets my ass down on

the counter. "Any chance your mother is going to walk in on us in the next fifteen minutes?"

"Fifteen minutes?"

"If I can't get you off in less time than that, I don't deserve you."

"I'll be the judge of what you deserve." I bite my lip as Logan hooks his fingers into the top of my yoga pants and pulls them down, urging me to lift my hips. "And I don't think my mother is coming home tonight."

There's no reason to play coy or deny him. I want this too fucking bad to play hard to get.

"Good." Logan claims my lips as my bare ass hits the cool laminate. His kiss is intoxicating, and my body hums with anticipation. I know he'll get me off with his talented tongue, and after yesterday, my body is primed for a release.

"Lean back, babe." He undoes the buttons on my oversized flannel and pulls down the cups of my tank top, sucking each nipple into his mouth as he moves swiftly down my body. I lean back on my elbows and watch him make quick work of laying me out like an all-you-can-eat buffet. He lifts my left thigh and hooks my knee with his bicep, propping my leg up on his shoulder while kissing the inside of my thigh.

Then he stops his ministrations to stare at my pussy spread wide for him. He smiles slowly and drags his eyes up my body to lock gazes with me. "You are like a fancy dessert plated up for me. One look and I know I'm going to be addicted to the rich, decadent taste of you."

This man and his swoon-worthy words. I've never

had a guy wax so poetic for me. Never had a man try to seduce my mind as well as my body.

He keeps his gaze locked with mine and lowers his head, his tongue running a long, lavish swipe up my center. I shudder, a small moan escaping my lips, and let my head drop back—my eyes closing.

That is all the signal he needs, plunging his tongue between my pussy lips, sucking my labia between his teeth. He swirls circles around my clit, flicking the engorged bud until I'm rolling my hips and riding his perfect mouth. Logan uses the wide expanse of his chest to push my legs further apart—one hand holding up my thigh, my other leg braced on his shoulder—and works me with only his tongue, teeth, and lips. It takes mere minutes for my orgasm to build and crash over. I have nothing soft to clutch, my fingernails scraping against the laminate as my pussy pulses and floods his mouth with cum.

"Oh fuck." I throw my head back, smacking it on the edge of the countertop.

Logan growls between my thighs, his mouth and tongue working me through my release until I'm so sensitive that I have no choice but to grab a fist full of his hair and push him off of me. "Please stop."

He grabs my hand and presses a kiss to my palm, chuckling softly. "Can you orgasm multiple times?"

"If I can, I never have before."

"Hmmm. Something we'll have to work toward when I move to town." He winks at me when I bring up eyes to his.

"You made me come in less than five minutes, so I guess you deserve me." Logan shakes his head and helps me sit up, my leg muscles shaking in post-orgasmic bliss.

"I don't deserve you yet, Tess, but hopefully you'll give me a chance to prove how good we can be together."

"You've definitely earned that chance." I wrap my ankles around the back of his thighs as he steps forward to kiss my lips, my scent all over his mouth. Sliding my fingers into his waistband, I move to unbuckle his belt, but he stops me by wrapping his fingers around mine.

"Not tonight, babe."

"But... don't you want to come, too?"

"I got exactly what I wanted tonight." He kisses me chastely and leans down, guiding my feet back into my yoga pant legs. "Now I can leave town with the taste of you burned into my memory."

It's at that moment a key slides into my front door. Logan quickly pulls up my yoga pants before my mom enters the house. The two of us lean casually against the countertop as she comes around the corner, a coy smile on her lips. "I have work tomorrow, so I had to come home, but I'm going straight to bed."

Logan shakes his head. "I was just leaving. I have an early morning flight, but I'll be back soon."

"Maybe we can have dinner when you get back?" My mom looks at me hopefully.

I roll my eyes and nod.

"I'd like that." Logan turns and kisses me chastely again. "I'll call you tomorrow, babe."

And just like that, the man of my dreams walks out of my life.

How am I going to survive however many weeks without him?

Waking up the next day, I grab my phone to check the time. It is ten a.m.—my normal wake-up time—but there are no text messages from Logan.

Was he running late this morning or did he forget me already?

My body thrums with need after the small taste of pleasure he gave me last night, and I can't wait for him to come back so I can show him some of my talents.

Why hasn't he texted yet?

Sighing, I roll out of bed, slide on a pair of sweatpants, a tank top, and an oversized hoodie, and relieve myself before slipping my bare feet into a pair of thick faux sheepskin boots. If he doesn't text me by this afternoon, I'll text him to make sure he made it to California okay.

If he doesn't text after that... I don't know what to think.

Brit stretches and performs a full body shake before she heads to the door and sits underneath her leash, her squishy muzzle and sad puppy dog eyes willing me to brave the frosty morning air.

Just as I'm pulling my knit cap down over my ears, I hear my phone chirp with an incoming message.

Good morning, babe.

Hope you've slept well and dreamed about me. I wasn't sure if you silenced your phone at night, and I didn't want to risk waking you up this morning by messaging too early. I've landed at LAX and have been thinking of you every step of the way. Can't wait to have you in my arms again, my lips pressed against your skin, your taste on my tongue.

I'll call you tonight. Logan.

Grabbing Brit's leash, I hook her collar and grab her soft muzzle, the smile on my face a mile wide. "He checked in, Brit. What should I text back?"

Brit's eyes go from me to the door and back to me as if to say, *I have to pee, Mom!*

"You're right. I should keep it simple." I say as we step out into the cold temperatures. While it was nice yesterday, a cold front moved in late last night, promising snow later this week, which makes me wish I was in Southern California with Logan.

Not that he invited me.

Not that I could afford a last-minute ticket.

We have so much to learn about each other, so maybe it's a good thing that we are getting to know each other long distance. I've never been good at postponing the physical, and I suppose that's because I've never really wanted to get to know the man I'm dating. If I don't really know him, then I can't fall in love.

Right?

Another text message chirps as Brit finishes up her business and we dump the evidence in a park trash can. I'm pulling my phone out of my pocket when I hear and then feel the rumble of 425 horsepower creeping up behind us. Reluctantly, I turn to see Dave driving his classic 1970 Challenger—one of several classic cars his father owns—through the parking lot adjacent to the field. He pulls up and parks next to the sidewalk I use to walk home, leaving me no choice but to pass him and acknowledge his existence.

He exits his vehicle and leans against the hood with his arms crossed over his chest, his lips curled into a frown. It strikes me as funny because I swear I've seen this pose in a movie, although I can't think of which one at the moment.

"What do you want?" I grumble, keeping a good eight feet of distance between us. He adores Brit, but I refuse to give him the satisfaction of her freely given love. Plus, I have a strong desire to punch him in his smug face after the comments he made to Logan in front of everyone.

"What you did Saturday was not cool, Tess. Do you have any idea how embarrassing it was to have our friends see you with another guy?"

"Our friends?" I scoff. "You mean your friends because my friends would never stand by and lie while you were out fucking other women!"

Dave rolls his eyes. "Oh please. I was drunk and the

nurse at the bar meant nothing. I don't even know her name. How many times do I have to tell you that?"

"Like she was the first or the last." I shake my head. "And if you really don't know her name, then that's just fucking sad. You threw away everything on a chick whose name you didn't even know."

Dave meets my anger with silence, knowing damn well there isn't a thing he can say to justify his actions.

He pushes off the hood and takes a step toward me. "How long are you going to slum around with the Army guy?"

I put my hand up and shake my head. "Don't you dare come near me."

He growls, his lips curling. "This is fucking bullshit, Tess. It shouldn't matter who I fucked in the past—we weren't married."

"Oh, but a ring on your finger will change everything?"

Why am I having this conversation? I don't want forever with him. I never did. Nothing he says will change my mind, so why am I giving him an ounce of hope by fighting with him?

More silence.

Dave tries for the soft approach, the one that used to work on me. "What do you want me to do, sweetheart? I'll buy you whatever you want. Take you wherever you want to go. Set a date and I'll throw you the most beautiful wedding you've ever dreamed of having. You know we're not over. No one deserves you like I do. No one can take care of you like I can."

Shaking my head, I turn with Brit and walk away. "Go home, Dave, and don't come around here again. You and I are done, and that is final."

Halfway down the block, Dave roars past us, driving way too fast for a residential area. That's okay, though. One thing about him, he'll throw a tantrum like a spoiled child, but he isn't violent.

Honestly, I'm not sure he even knows how to throw a punch.

His friends, on the other hand, have gotten into quite a few scuffles over the years that I've known him, and I don't trust them at all. They are like devoted dogs, willing to do anything for a treat.

Once we're back in the house, I unleash and feed Brit before pulling my phone out of my pocket. I plop down on the couch to find the missed text I received while walking around the park was from Dave.

Skip, ignore, silence.

I'm tempted to delete it, but I skip down to Logan's message and reply instead.

> I'm glad you made it to LA safely. Have fun with your family. I work tonight, so if I don't answer, that will be why.

> What time do you get off work?

> I close every night this week, although the bar closes early Sunday through Wednesday. I should be home between midnight and one.

My phone rings, and Logan's number appears on my screen.

Smiling, I answer. "Couldn't wait to hear my voice, huh?"

"Couldn't risk not talking to you tonight," he answers, his voice a little rough. "How did you sleep?"

"Great. A good orgasm usually knocks me right out." I grin, my exchange with Dave instantly forgotten.

Logan chuckles. "I'll keep that in mind. Meanwhile, I tossed and turned all night."

"You should have let me take care of you before you left." I'm pretty sure he's in a car, as the road noise is too loud for a sidewalk cafe. The fact that he has an audience makes me want to tease him as much as possible.

"I can wait."

"Can you wait six weeks? That's a long time, Logan."

"You forget, babe. I've deployed for eight to twelve-months many times over the years. Six weeks is nothing."

I don't know why, but his restraint is a turn-on. Is he this disciplined about everything in his life? Is this a side-effect of his Army training? What other forms of restraint does he practice?

"Is it wrong that only makes me want you more?" I tease.

"Not in my mind."

"I wonder what you'd say if you didn't have an audience right now."

He chuckles. "You'll find out soon enough. What time do you leave for work?"

"Five thirty."

"I'll call you later, but if I miss you, call me when you get off work. Okay, babe?"

"I will do that. Talk to you later." I hang up and lean back on the couch cushions, sighing contently.

Falling head over heels for a guy is completely out of character, but something tells me I won't be able to resist Logan's charms, even if I want to. Part of me thinks I should harden my heart like I always do, but he feels different from all the others. Maybe it's the blue-collar, hard-working, disciplined military veneer he has. He's sweet and thoughtful—a total gentleman—but there's coiled power underneath his picture-perfect physique that I find dangerously attractive.

Maybe I've been dating entitled assholes for so long that I forgot what a normal man is like. I don't think I've ever spent time with a sweet and sexy guy, but to be honest, everyone I've wasted more than two weeks with has been surface level at best because I have also been surface level—just like my mother.

A pretty package unwilling to invest real feelings.

I always believed that when the right guy showed up, I'd inherently know it. Is this it? Are the butterflies dancing in my belly trying to tell me something?

He believes there's something here, so why shouldn't I?

At least with Logan we have something in common besides insane attraction. He's a working stiff like me, and won't think I'm using him for his money or the places we can go or things he can buy me. It would be nice to know a man wants me to want him for who he is, and not what he can give me.

An opportunity to prove I'm more than a "gold digger"—a moniker I've heard throughout my life.

A scarlet letter I'm tired of wearing.

VETERAN
K9
TEAM
REPORTING
FOR DUTY

Chapter 7
Logan

"Who was that?" Levi asks with a stupid grin on his face. He and his twin, my other brother Lennox—or Knox, as he's known on the big screen—keep their hair a shaggy length that I now admire after years of high and tight.

"My girlfriend."

"Since when do you have a girlfriend? Don't tell me you met someone before leaving Washington."

"She's not in Washington. She's in Colorado."

His eyes snap to mine. "I thought you were visiting Army buddies."

I glance at the road and shrug. My family assumed I would come home once my enlistment was up, and although I've had other plans for quite some time, I've never corrected their assumptions. "I was, then I met her. Even if I hadn't, I was planning to move to Spring City, anyway."

"What? Why?" Levi merges onto I-10 toward Malibu.

"Where are you going? I thought we were meeting at Gram's house." Even though our grandmother died nearly fifteen years ago, in my mind, the house we lived in most of my life was always hers.

"The 'rents want to host Thanksgiving at the Malibu house." He shrugs. "Back to Colorado. Why aren't you coming home?"

"What makes this home?"

"Uh, I don't know… all of your family is here." He flashes me an exasperated look that I know is fake. If he could live anywhere, I doubt this would be the place. It would probably be some small island in the Pacific. As long as he could surf, he'd be pretty happy.

"Besides Knox, how often do you see the family? Three or four times a year?"

"I catch up with Selyne once or twice a month."

"That's because you are the most thoughtful of all of us. This simple fact is that you're here because of your career, and maybe because of Knox, who is also here because of his career. Are you telling me you couldn't find a dozen other places to live happily?"

He shakes his head, turning onto the PCH. "Mom is not going to be happy that you aren't coming back to the nest."

I shrug, my eyes glued to the blue ocean waters and white froth beating the rocks below. "What can she do about it? I'm twenty-five. Her last leash on me disintegrated months ago."

Levi says nothing as we drive for the next ten minutes in relative silence. It's only when he turns off the highway onto our residential street that he pulls over and puts the convertible into park. "I wouldn't be so sure about that, Logan."

"So sure about what?" I turn in my seat to face him.

"Even if our grandparents established our trusts, Mom is the executor, and she's crafty enough to make your life a living hell to get it." He runs his hand through his shaggy locks, smoothing out some tangles from the open road air. "Over the years she's made comments—usually at the family get-togethers where you've been absent—about how you will eventually come back home or she'll cut you off. If you had enlisted for another tour, I'm sure she'd be pulling some shenanigans no matter what. But you exit the Army and don't come home—" he shakes his head "—I don't think that will go over well."

"Did she put stipulations on you and Knox? Selyne?"

He does this half-shake, half-nod thing with his head. "Not exactly. What she said was that Hollywood money created our trust funds, and therefore we deserve them because we are keeping the Mejer name relevant. Also, the funds pay out in installments over the next five years, so even if she can't stop you from collecting today, she might fuck with the amount and hold this over you for years."

"Fuck." I turn away and stare at the landscape. If I wasn't looking at investing in the VKC, I would begrudgingly turn away from my trust fund just to spite my mother, but now I have other people counting on this money—and me.

"Who knows? She could surprise us. But you've done a damn good job of staying away for the last six years, and I don't think she's going to let that slide."

I frown and turn on him. "I've seen all of you at least once per year. It's not like I fell off the face of the earth and disowned you."

"Your last name is Pratt, man." Levi raises his brow and then puts the car in gear, letting that be the last word on the subject.

I walk into the house like I'm sweeping the ground for land mines and searching the corners for sniper attacks. I get all the way into the living room overlooking the ocean when my sister jumps up from her seat, rushing toward me with her arms spread wide. "Hellraiser!"

Selyne flings her body against mine, wrapping her arms around my neck and her legs around my waist, way too confident I will catch her.

"Jesus, Brat. One day, I'm not going to catch you."

"Liar." She kisses my cheek and then squeezes the breath out of me, putting her lips near my ear. "I missed you too much."

Fuck, fuck, fuck. Add a mushy sister to my impending guilt trip, and I'm regretting this visit. I mean, I love my brothers and sister, and despite all our differences, I even love my mom and dad, but their lifestyle is not something I want to welcome into my world. "I missed you, too."

"There he is." Knox comes around the corner with a

giant protein shake in his hand, Langston right behind him.

Jesus—it's been six and a half years since the five of us have been in the same room at the same time. The last time I saw them was the night after my high school graduation, when I came home from the prison/boarding school my mother had shipped me off to during my freshman year. One stolen high-performance sports car, a high-speed chase, and a little over one hundred grand in damages added to a handful of underage drinking, truancy, and noise complaints put me on the other side of the country at Silverton Gables Academy for the next four years—the school my father attended before Harvard Business.

My sister drops her legs and lets me go in time for Knox—all two hundred and ten pounds of him—to wrap me in a bear hug. Knox and Levi are twenty-nine and blond like me, while my sister is weeks away from turning twenty-seven and the only brunette in the family. Langston offers me his hand and pulls me in for a quick hug. He's a big-time director responsible for three of the top ten action films in the last twenty years. For someone who is only thirty-two years old, it's quite an accomplishment. Of course, my brother Knox has starred in two of those three films, with his twin, Levi, as lead stuntman and now the stunt coordinator.

Of the five of us, Langston is the oldest and was away at college when I got into all of my trouble. Even Knox and Levi were out of high school and Selyne's education was done via tutors while she traveled around the world doing the modeling gig.

"Are you out?" Langston clasps his hand on my shoulder and guides me to the couch.

"Not yet." I glance around, wondering where Mom and Dad are, before reluctantly plopping down onto the cushion. "I'll outprocess in the next couple of weeks."

"And then?" Knox asks at the same time Levi walks in with two Vitamin waters. He tosses me one but says nothing, letting me answer the burning question of the day.

"And then," I pause and take a deep breath, cracking open the bottle and taking a deep drink before answering. "I'm moving to Colorado."

Knox and Levi exchange a look while Langston does nothing more than stare at me.

Selyne sits next to me and draws her long legs up underneath her. "You really don't want to come home, do you?"

I sigh. "It's got nothing to do with the family."

That's only a partial lie.

"Besides, how often are you around, anyway? Us spending time together has nothing to do with where I live. Meanwhile, a handful of the soldiers I served with have settled in Spring City, and they're involved in a worthy business venture that I want to invest in. Plus, there's a woman."

Levi chuckles. "Isn't there always?"

"You've met someone?" Selyne perks up. "Tell us about her."

"There's not a lot to tell except that I'm crazy about her. She's headstrong and beautiful and not likely to put up with my shit."

"What does she think of your family?" Knox asks.

Guilt punches me in the gut, and my eyes slide to Levi. "I haven't told her yet."

Langston crosses his arms over his chest. "So, you're moving to Spring City for a woman who doesn't know who you really are."

I'm on the verge of telling him off when my mother and father walk into the room.

"Logan, you're home." My father opens his arms wide as I push myself off the couch. He's a good man— the peacekeeper of the family—the quiet, geeky, and subdued escort to my mother, who craves notoriety, fame, and all the paparazzi flashing lights that go along with it.

He's showered her with love and affection from the moment they met and has been her devoted lapdog for the last thirty-five years. There was a time when I hated him for it. I couldn't understand why—from my juvenile standpoint—he let her walk all over him, and because of that, I didn't respect him.

Now that I've met Tess, I think I understand him a little better. At least I understand the desire to raise someone on a pedestal and worship them. Only, I don't think Tess would ever walk all over me. That's just not her style.

"Hey Dad." My father is small compared to all of his boys, and I easily engulf him in my hug.

"You look good, son." He slaps my back with his open palms.

"And where is my greeting?" My mother stands there in all her glamorous glory with her hands on her hips. She is a true timeless beauty who has had little cosmetic surgery over the years. Maybe a filler here and there, but no time under the knife, which is unheard of in Hollywood. Although she is approaching sixty, she could easily pass for someone in their mid-thirties.

My father, Burton, lets me go with a sigh.

"Hey Mom." I wrap my arms around Loretta, trying to feel some of the love she swears she has for me on the rare occasions we talk on the phone. While I've seen my brothers and sister at random locations around the world over the last six years of my life—including austere locations while deployed overseas—I haven't seen my parents in a couple of years.

She pats my biceps softly and pushes me away from her. "I'm happy you finally made it to a family get-together. I assume you're here for your trust fund?"

I inhale deeply and plaster a placating smile on my face. "Amongst other things."

"Well, Walter will be here at three with the paperwork." My mother says casually, turning her attention to the catering staff as they bring in an assortment of healthy snacks. "Karen prepped your room. Why don't you unpack and get settled? We can catch you up on all the family gossip later."

My mother lifts her hand over her head and calls out to one of the staff members, giving herself a welcome distraction and a reason to leave the room. My eyes slide in Levi's direction, who answers me with an imperceptible shake of his head.

"It's good to have you home, son." Dad reaches out and squeezes my shoulder, his passive nature evident in his resigned sigh. "How about we go for a drive tomorrow?"

"Sounds good, Dad."

My siblings watch in silence as my parents exit the room, filling up small plates and grabbing drinks while thanking the staff. Once they are gone, Selyne jumps up and hooks her arm in mine. "Let's put on our suits, lounge by the pool, soak up the sun, and catch up."

I let my sister pull me down the hallway and drop me off at my room. "Meet you outside."

My bag is sitting on the bed. I guess Levi grabbed it while I wasn't paying attention and dumped it in my room. I'm a little numb after twenty minutes of interaction with my family, my black sheep status renewed with vigor by everything left unsaid. It doesn't matter what I've done, where I've been, the lives I've saved by my actions—I'll never fit in or be accepted by my mother.

Unfortunately, in this household, my mother's word is gospel.

And we're not even religious.

Unzipping my bag, I rifle through my clothing to find a pair of board shorts. Any clothes I left behind will be way too small for me now. I grew another two inches after high school and put on thirty pounds of muscle between boot camp, AIT, and deployments, with nothing better to do than lift with my brethren.

There's a knock on my door and Levi pops his head in. "Hey man, do you need a pair of trunks?"

"No, I got some." I walk out of the adjoining bathroom in my shorts, shirtless.

His eyes skim over my chest. "No tats, eh?"

"Not yet. The temptation is there. I mean, most of the guys have them, but I haven't figured out what I want."

He tosses me a towel and we walk out the patio doors, facing the pool deck and pergolas.

"You got big, baby bro. You could join my ranks and body double for Knox when his pretty face isn't needed." Levi smirks as Knox turns to face us, his eyes narrowed.

"Fuck you." Knox offers me a beer, the first of what I suspect will be many over the next five days. I wouldn't have voluntarily come for so many days if not for the holiday and the fact that Walter is going away with his family tomorrow through the weekend.

"Tell us about this business you want to invest in, Logan," Knox says as he lowers himself into the hot tub.

Levi and I follow, the water just warm enough to be comfortable under the bright blue November sky. Langston is nowhere to be seen, and Selyne is on the phone at the other end of the pool.

"It's a dog kennel and training facility run by veterans primarily for active duty military. They want to grow the facility by training military-grade working dogs for law enforcement, and PTSD support animals for qualifying combat veterans." I shrug. "I worked with these guys in the field, and this is about more than making money. It's about giving back to the men and women who need it."

"What's your investment look like?" Levi asks.

"A couple million, I guess. I want to buy the land surrounding their existing property and build on it."

"Are you going to become a dog trainer?" Knox eyes me almost comically. We never had animals we cared for, which is why I want my own after I'm settled. I've wanted a Boxer since I was seven years old. While we had the resources to have whatever we wanted growing up, dog hair was something my mother wouldn't tolerate.

"No. I don't have the skills to train dogs, especially these kinds of dogs. I figured I'd run the business side of growing the operation with the current owner."

"What do you know about land development?" Levi tips back his bottle and downs the last of his beer that I've yet to touch.

Jesus—talking to these two is like being the ball into the middle of the ping-pong tournament. "Nothing, but money will put me in contact with the right people, don't you think?"

"I suppose." Knox shrugs. "Tell me something, Logan. If you aren't homesick, why separate from the military? Why not do twenty with your green family?"

I can taste the bitterness on his tongue, and it surprises me. Outside of my mother, who only seems to care because of how my military service reflected on the family, I didn't think my siblings gave a shit about any of it.

Subconsciously, I grab my beer bottle and down the cool liquid in a couple of rapid gulps. Setting down the empty, I shake my head and mutter under my breath. "Can't do it anymore. Not after last February."

"What happened last February?" Levi asks, and I remember who I'm sitting with. My brothers, my blood family, the ones I have left in the dark on all the bullshit that has gone down over the years.

I stare at the water bubbling in the center, the color of the lights at our feet changing. It's loud, and yet the silence between us is deafening. At one time, I craved a genuine relationship with my brothers, like the one I have with my brethren, but as part of keeping a low profile, I've kept my real-world experiences as far away from them as possible.

Licking my lips, I bring my eyes up to meet theirs, only then realizing that tears are streaming down my cheeks. "I lost someone while on patrol. We almost lost a second. It happened so fast, and there was nothing I could do but take cover and return fire until we eliminated the threat. I can't do that again. I can't watch another person's brother, son, or husband die in front of me."

Levi is up, pulling me to my feet, and wrapping his arms around me before I realize he's moved. "We had no idea, man."

Knox joins us, cocooning me on the other side. "Fuck, Logan. I'm not sure if I've ever said it, but I'm proud of you for taking your own path and involving yourself in something bigger than this family."

My brothers let go of me, and I shake my head. "I don't think any of you have ever told me you're proud of me before."

"May not have said it, but definitely have thought it many times over the years." Knox ruffles my hair and sits down at the same time Levi lets me go.

"I want to ask why you didn't tell us, but I guess I know why," Levi says.

I nod. "Don't tell anyone else. Mom and Dad, Selyne and Langston don't need to be burdened with the gory details of my life. Okay?"

Knox and Levi exchange a look. "Only if you promise that if you ever need us, you'll call. And if you need someone to talk to about all of this, even if it's not us, you will."

"I promise."

"Were any of the guys in Colorado involved last February?" Levi asks.

"Yeah, a couple of them." I pick at the label on my empty beer bottle. Karden was the one to take the sniper out. Saint was standing beside me, returning fire while Bishop screamed and clung to Miller's lifeless body.

Sometimes I wake up to the sound of him screaming in my head, but I'm working through it.

Knox licks his lips. "I guess I understand why you feel more connected to them than us, but understand, little brother, we don't like it this way."

Levi nods. "We miss you."

I smile. "I miss you, too. Once I'm out and settled somewhere, we can be more intentional with our visits."

"Maybe we can come out and meet some of your fellow soldiers."

"I think you'd like them."

"I'm sure we would." Levi tilts his chin and lifts his empty bottle in Selyne's direction as she walks toward us. "Can you grab three more?"

She rolls her eyes. "So glad to have my brothers together, so I have someone to wait on."

"Brat." I flash her a smile.

"Hellraiser." She hands me all three bottles and then sits cross-legged on the pool deck. "What did I miss?"

No way in hell I'm filling her in on any of our conversations. The less she knows, the better. Even though I know my sister loves me, she is my mother's puppet and would do nothing to gain Loretta's disapproval. In many ways, I think our mother lives vicariously through Selyne. She's the star my mother never became. "You were telling me about your worldwide adventures. Where are you off to next?"

"Ugh." She rolls her eyes. "That's who I was on the phone with. I'm doing a fashion show in Dubai, and my agent is negotiating my fees for Doha and Saudi Arabia. These happen after New York, London, and Paris, of course."

"Of course." Levi rolls his eyes.

I frown. "I really wish you'd skip Saudi."

She pats my arm with a placating smile on her lips, as if to tell me to mind my own business. I haven't been around to advise her over the years, so I have no right to do so now.

"Let's go out tonight," she chirps. "We haven't been out together in a long time, and Logan has never been to any of the private clubs. Let's show him what he's missing."

My brothers shrug. "Sounds fine to us."

As my brothers and sister prattle on about the most recent gossip amongst their celebrity peers—most of whom I've never met—I lean back in the tub and let my mind wander. I wonder what the guys will think when I finally confirm the rumors by introducing them to my blockbuster action star brothers or supermodel sister? Will they put pieces together from their memories and change their opinion of me once they realize I was never scraping by from one paycheck to another?

What will Tess think about all of this? When it's all said and done, will she care?

While we are getting to know each other and doing the long-distance thing, I want to shower her with affection. I'd like to send her flowers, but considering her history with Dave, would she find my intentions charming or a turnoff?

I stare at Selyne while she talks and wonder if she'd ever date a man with a net worth of less than a hundred million. I'm sure if she tried, our mother would ruin it.

Shit. I won't get any good advice from my family. They don't know how to relate to people who grew up with nothing or continue to struggle today. I'll stick with what my gut tells me, which is to make sure Tess knows she's special.

VETERAN
K9
TEAM
REPORTING
FOR DUTY

Chapter 8
Tess

5:12pm: Can't call right now, but I've been thinking about you all afternoon. Have a good night at work and please call me when you get home. <3

8:27pm: Going to dinner with my siblings and then to some local hot spot. I'll have my phone on me, so don't think twice about calling when you can.

10:43pm: God, I'm full. Amazing food, but I ate too much and something tells me I'm going to drink too much tonight. I know you like Thai food, but do you like seafood?

I can't wait to take you out on a proper date and find out about all the foods you like and dislike.

10:58pm: Damn, I fucking miss you. Is that crazy? It feels a little bonkers to miss someone I just met, but I know what I feel. Can't wait to see you again, Tess. Touch you, kiss you, hold you.

> Yeah, as much as I want to do other things, right now I'd love nothing more than to hold you until all the problems of the world melt away.

S taring down at my most recent message, I can't help but smile. Maybe I should be creeped out by Logan's bold declaration. I'm certainly no stranger to love-bombing. Dave did it every time he sensed I was on the verge of breaking up with him.

Instead of warning bells, my heart swells as I type out a response.

> 10:59pm: I miss you, too. Yes, it's crazy. We just met, and we don't really know each other. Not really. But that doesn't stop me from missing you, too.

Dawn hip-checks me back into reality. "What has you desperately checking your phone all night? A new beau?"

"I think so." A light blush hits my cheeks.

She grins. "About time you met a new guy. The old one sucked."

I chuckle. "Yeah, I know."

"It's quiet tonight, nothing I can't handle by myself. If you want to head home to your man, I can cover the bar."

Sighing, I shake my head and the sappy feeling infusing my chest away. I can't imagine rushing home to my man night after night. Actually, I can—and that's the scary part. Could that be my future? "He's in California with his family for the holiday, but if you don't need me, I wouldn't mind taking off an hour early."

"Get your butt home, girl. See you tomorrow night." Dawn smiles and flings a towel in my direction as her fiancé, Corey, takes a seat at the bar. She's been in love with him since they were kids, but he only recently pulled his head out of his ass. I will give him credit, though. Since he figured out that she's the love of his life, he's been a devoted boyfriend and I'm sure will be an amazing husband and eventually father.

"Same bat time, same bat channel." I smack the counter in front of Corey and grab my purse from under the till. "See you guys tomorrow."

In my car, I place my phone in its cradle and call Logan. He answers on the second ring, but the noise surrounding him is too loud to hear him clearly. "Give me a second to find a quiet place."

I stand by and wait. He's clearly at a club where the music pumps through the walls and the floors vibrate from the dancing feet.

"Logan, where are you going?" A female's voice calls out.

I don't hear his response, if there is one, but my stomach clenches just the same.

Shit. Don't be a jealous bitch, Tess. Just cool your jets and give him the benefit of the doubt.

Besides, you just met. He owes you nothing.

The ambient noise dies and a car door slams shut. "That's better. Hey, babe."

"Hi."

"You got off work early?"

"I did. It was a slow night. Where are you?" I try to keep the accusatory tone out of my voice.

"We're at some club. I'm not sure which one. It's good to hear your voice. I guess my text messages didn't turn you off?"

"Not even a little bit."

Logan sighs, and it sounds bone weary. "I wish you were here."

"Are you okay?"

"Just family, you know? I mean, I love them, and being here reminds me I miss my brothers and sister, but I also know living here wouldn't be the same as visiting. Plus, they are giving me shit for not moving home."

"Are you thinking about moving to California instead of Colorado?" I ask softly, disappointment settling in my stomach.

"No," he says with absolute certainty. "I'm coming to Colorado. Everything I want in my future is there."

A huge smile spreads across my lips, but I say nothing.

He sighs. "You asked me if I can wait six weeks."

"Yeah?"

"Can and will are two very different things. I will wait as long as I have to for you, but if I can see you sooner, I'll do that. Who knows, maybe I'll fly back to Washington via Colorado later this week."

I giggle. "Maybe I'll tuck myself into bed every night

wearing something sexy, just in case an early morning visitor wants to wake me up."

"Mmmm. Maybe I'll have some things sent to you."

A salacious grin plumps my cheeks. "What's your favorite color, Logan? Maybe I already have something you'll like."

"No offense, babe. But any lingerie that dickhead bought you, I'm burning." His voice deepens, a dark sense of possessiveness laced through his words. "And I'll replace it."

I sigh. He's right. Of course, he's right.

"I guess we'll cross that bridge when we come to it." Any sense of possessiveness should turn me off, but with Logan, it feels more like claiming versus owning. Dave wanted everyone to see me as his possession, but I believe Logan just wants me to be his, damn what everyone else thinks.

It's a subtle distinction, but one I feel deep in my soul.

"I guess we will. Where are you right now? Are you home safe in bed?"

"No, I'm sitting in my car in the parking lot of the bar."

"Jesus, Tess. Are your doors locked?" He huffs his annoyance.

I glance over at my door locks and quietly push the plunger down. "They are now."

"I'm not saying you can't take care of yourself, but I hate you being out late, in the dark, in a bar parking lot. It's not safe, babe."

The security staff at the Last Stand are the best in the city. Max has cameras pointed in every direction of the parking lot, and I'm betting someone was watching me walk from the back door to my car. If anyone else was out here, I'm betting Corey or Denny would have been on the guy before I ever saw them.

But Logan has a point, and I'm happy to have his concern.

"Okay, starting my car now and heading home. Keep me company while I drive?"

"Yeah."

We talk on my drive home. With every question I ask about his family, his answers become more and more vague. So far, I know he has three brothers—two of which are twins—and one sister who is only fourteen months older than him. They all live in Southern California, but exactly where, I'm still not sure.

Logan keeps saying Los Angeles, but is that city or county? Even with my limited knowledge of the area, I know the county has dozens of cities and millions of people.

"Do you have any nieces or nephews?" I ask, trying to pry a little more information out of him.

"No. Everyone is single." He yawns, which makes me yawn. "Are you home yet?"

"I just pulled into the driveway. Mom's not here, which isn't a surprise."

"Brit will be happy to see you walk through the door."

"Yeah, I'll have to take her for a walk. Why don't you go back inside the club and call me later?"

"I think I'm going to talk my brother into taking me home. I'm just not feeling it tonight. When I get back to the house, I'll call and tell you a bedtime story."

"Sounds great."

VETERAN
K9
TEAM
REPORTING
FOR DUTY

Chapter 9
Logan

"Hey." I answer my phone when I see Levi's number on the screen. I left California two weeks ago and returned to our normal radio silence. My mother's caustic tongue lashed out at me every chance she got while I was home, which is why my siblings did their best to shield me by taking me out as often as possible. We went shopping, hiking, surfing, and ate out at a different hot spot every night. No doubt there were pictures taken of my siblings, but I can only hope my sunglasses and occasional baseball hat obscured my face.

It's so dumb. This is not the life I signed up for, and it's not the one I want, but my mother made it very clear that the only way I'm getting my hands on my trust fund is if I embrace the Mejer name and use it to further solidify our place as Hollywood royalty.

I have no idea how to do that and still get what I want.

"You have a minute to talk in private?" Levi says, a host of voices sounding off behind him. I'm guessing he's on a movie set or inside the studio or somewhere business is taking place.

"Yeah." I'm working desk duty as I final out of the military, running to random appointments as most of my fellow soldiers get things ready for the holidays and the next deployment coming in February. "Let me run to my car."

"Knox, let's duck in here." Levi calls to our brother, letting me know this isn't some bullshit session. This call just got a lot more interesting, because I never get a call from both of them, except on the holidays.

"What's up?" I say from the privacy of my car.

"We have an idea for you—a solution to your trust fund problems with Mom," Knox says, all the external noise gone.

Exhaling slowly, I stare out the window at the red brick and sand colored buildings and pine trees dotting the landscape on Ft. Lewis. I did not leave California feeling warm and fuzzy about our mother. "I'm listening."

"You've seen John Wick 3? The scene where the Belgian Malinois are tearing up shit?"

"Yeah."

"Do you think the K9 trainers in Colorado could train dogs like that?"

I shake my head, realizing they can't see me. "I don't know."

Knox sighs. "I talked to Brady—he's the animal

trainer from my last film—and military working dogs are in high demand right now. Production companies are looking to include them more and more in action films like the ones I star in. If my brother had a company that provided these trained beasts to blockbuster action films —and he named the company Mejer something or other —then he would fulfill all of our mother's requirements to access his trust fund."

"You could run it out of Colorado, Logan. The dogs and trainers don't have to be there, not all of them anyway, just the company. Maybe you have your office in one building on the property with your buddies. You know?" Levi adds. "This is an easy way to get everything you want while giving Mom what she wants."

"She'll never go for it." I finally say after thinking through what they're saying and trying to envision what it could look like.

"You let us work Mom," Knox says. "We'll slip it into conversation this weekend. Langston's on board."

"He is?" That surprises me. Langston was out of the house and away at college before I was a teenager, so we were never close.

"Yeah. We'll talk about the need and Levi will throw in a 'aren't those the kinds of dogs Logan's buddies in Colorado train' into the conversation." Knox chuckles. "And he says he's not an actor."

"I didn't say I couldn't act. I'm just better at throwing myself head first out of windows," Levi shoots back.

I shake my head. "I guess I need to talk to the team in Colorado."

"I'll text you Brady's information. He can fill you in with what you need to establish a reputable business in this arena," Knox says at the same time voices break into the background. "Shit. Gotta go. We'll call you Sunday night."

"Sounds good. Thanks." I sit in my car in a stunned silence, surprised my brothers will help me given the situation. They could easily turn their backs on me, as I did them all those years ago. If I think back on it, they've always put in the extra effort to connect with me. When I was deployed, Levi was the one who contacted my commander and asked for a favor, getting me a seventy-two hour pass. Knox came and met the troops as part of that favor, with my sister signing suggestive headshots to guys in my platoon. Talk about embarrassing—seeing my sister in a pinup-esque red, white, and blue bikini plastered up on wall lockers around the compound. And because I kept my familial connection under wraps, I couldn't exactly go around and tear them down like I wanted to.

At least, not when anyone was looking.

I pull up my texting app to send a message to Janey when I see the last interchange I had with Tess last night.

> My personal alarm clock. I love it. Just a
> few more weeks, handsome. Then you
> are all mine.

Fuck calling.

This is a conversation I should have with the team in person, considering it affects all of them. I pull up my travel agent's number and tell her to book me the next flight to Denver and a car.

Then I message Janey.

> Can I meet with you and the team at the
> center tonight?

> Sure. What's up?

> A bit of a development regarding my
> investment, but I have a plan and I want
> complete buy-in considering you said
> everyone is an owner.

> They are. What time do you get in?
> Need a ride?

> Nah. I'll get a car. My flight lands around
> five thirty, so I guess I'll be there around
> seven?

> Around that. We'll order some food and
> wait for you.

> See you then.

It's Thursday night—ladies' night at the Last Stand— so I know Tess is working. Instead of telling her I'm coming, I think I'll surprise her and book us a suite downtown. My woman needs to be pampered, and it's time for me to deliver on all the promises I've made to her mind and body.

After I tell her the truth about my family.

Then, once I'm settled in Spring City, I'll deliver the unspoken promises I've made to her heart.

I pull up to the VKC, a half-dozen cars in the parking lot. The sun set hours ago, but the night sky out here is bright, with millions of stars and a rising moon shining overhead. I swear, it's like being in the desert, the sky uncluttered by city lights or LA pollution.

As soon as I open the front door, Janey yells from the conference room. "We're in here."

It looks like the entire team is here, sans Saint, who won't be here until March or April at the earliest. Everyone stands and I slap palms with Kemp, Vale, and Barron while tilting my chin in Linc and Karden's direction on the other side of the table.

Janey pats an empty chair next to her. "Want a beer?"

"Yeah, sounds good." I take a seat.

Karden shoves a to-go container of tacos in my direction. "What's going on, Hollywood?"

I snort and take the cold beer offered to me. "Funny you should call me that. I have a confession, not that some of you will be surprised."

For the next fifteen minutes, I give them headlines, admitting my connection to the Mejer family and why I felt the need to bury it in the press all of these years.

"I fucking knew it. You look just like Knox Mejer." Linc grins.

Karden shrugs. "Makes sense why you hid it, though. I can't imagine being deployed with some of the knuckle-heads we've known and having them know."

"Yeah." I take a long drag of my beer. "I went home at Thanksgiving to sign the paperwork and release funds from my trust. That's the money I planned to invest in the center and start my civilian life away from home, but my mother has other ideas. She wants me to come home and join the family business, and therefore she's blocking my access."

"Planned?" Janey says softly, her disappointment obvious.

"I still plan, but it's changed a bit and might take me a few months longer than I expected to get things going." I glance around the room. "Have you ever thought of training dogs for action films?"

They all exchange a look while shaking their heads.

"Wouldn't even know how to go about it, man," Kemp says.

"I'm in contact with a guy, so if you are interested, you could be a part of it. Or, if you're not, it can be my thing alone. But, bare minimum, I'd need to establish the booking office here, maybe build a small training facility or something on the land I buy. Honestly, I'm not sure about the logistics yet, but we're thinking this might be a way to give my mother what she wants while giving me what I want, which in turn gets you what you need—capital investment."

"Who is we?" Janey asks.

"My brothers came up with this idea and called me earlier today. The trainer Knox put me in contact with worked on his last film, *Before Dawn*. He confirmed that the demand for military working dogs is high right now on action films."

I glance around the room at the men assembled. Linc shrugs but says nothing, turning his attention to peeling the label off his beer bottle. Barron, Karden, and Vale lean back in their chairs with their arms crossed over their chests, their eyes on Janey and Kemp. I know they aren't knee deep in the planning stages of VKC's future yet, even if they are stakeholders.

Janey bites her lip and exchanges a look with Kemp. "I don't know, Logan."

"Which part concerns you?" I respond with a lump in my throat. I thought about this on the flight over, and this is an easy solution for all.

"It's one thing to bring you on as a veteran and an investor, but it sounds like you're bringing your family in who we don't know. What if something happens to you and the family wants to take over your business dealings, which bleed into ours? I can't risk losing what we've built or will build, and I doubt we'll ever have the kind of money or power to fend them off if they came for us." She licks her lips. "No offense to your family."

"No offense taken—" I wave away her concerns "—

and I wouldn't let that happen. We'll use lawyers and make sure we're all protected. This is a means to an end, and maybe you'll see nothing more than a piece of mail with my business name on it, or maybe we'll train out of this location."

Linc shrugs again. "I wouldn't mind learning how to train dogs for movies. Some of those stunts are fucking cool."

A few of the other guys nod.

Grinning at Linc and Karden, I turn back to Janey. "We can work out the specifics, but right now I need to know if this is a deal breaker for you?"

"What if it is?" Barron asks, to my surprise.

I sigh. "If it is, then I'll find another way to get the money. It might take me a few months, which will delay buying the land, but I'll figure it out. Accepting or not accepting this business proposal doesn't change my commitment to what you are doing here or my desire to be a part of it."

Janey shakes her head. "It's not a deal breaker."

"Could be fun," Vale says.

Kemp nods. "As long as our primary mission stays focused on the military community and veterans, I'm down for whatever."

I return his nod. "It will."

"When will you know for sure?" Janey asks.

"Sunday night, Monday at the latest." I flip open the to-go container and grab a taco, my stomach no longer doing nervous flip-flops.

"When do you fly back to Washington?" Karden asks.

"Monday afternoon." I say around a mouth full of taco.

"Need a place to crash?" he offers.

"No. I got a room for me and Tess, but thanks for offering."

"Still going strong, eh?" Janey stands and clears her empty container.

"As strong as a long distance thing can go, considering we're still getting to know each other."

"Does she know about your family?" Linc raises his brow at the same time Vale stands up and clears his and Kemp's trash.

I take another long draw off my beer and empty the bottle before shaking my head. "Not yet. I'm going to tell her this weekend."

Vale grabs his phone and keys, his eyes on me. "Sorry, but I need to get home to my pregnant wife. Whatever I can do to help, just let me know."

"Thanks. I might bring the trainer out here to meet you guys, answer any question you have, et cetera."

"Sounds good." Vale salutes the room and walks out.

"Does she know you're here?" Karden asks as he grabs me another beer.

"No. I'm going to surprise her at work. I don't suppose you guys would like to come to the bar with me tonight?"

"I need to run home, drop Kiki off, and change clothes, but you could persuade me," Karden smirks.

"Yeah, yeah. Beers on me." I chuckle.

Linc nods and grabs his plate, throwing it away. "I'll run home, shower, grab Brandi, and meet you there. What do you say, Barron? Think Betty will come out?"

Barron's lip curls. "I suppose so, except that means I have to come out, too."

"Yes, old man. You'd have to leave the comfort of your couch and risk showing off your woman."

I'm surprised there are women considering three weeks ago Linc mentioned instructing hot ski bunnies, but whatever. It's not my place to poke or ask questions.

"I'll see if Mari wants to come out." Kemp smacks Janey on the arm. "What do you say, LaVey?"

She shrugs. "Why not? I'll meet you guys there."

We go our separate ways, and I stop by the grocery store on my way to my hotel, setting up the dozen red roses I bought on the desk near the door. Jumping into the shower, I quickly towel off and change before heading out, nabbing a solitary rose from the bundle. I'm sure Tess will have to work Friday and Saturday night, but I can deal with that as long as I'm waking up with her in my arms every morning.

Fuck—I hope she's okay with my family. I've spent the last three weeks letting her get to know the man I am away from all the bullshit. The man I spent the last six years cultivating away from the cushion of privilege.

But if I'm honest with myself, I've never really jumped without a financial parachute strapped to my back. I tried to live like my brethren, but deep down I knew if I got into trouble, I could tap into my savings that's been in place since I was born. It's not millions, but it's certainly more than most of the men I've deployed with will ever save.

Do I have to live like a pauper to get the girl?

I don't see how that would serve either of us, or the life I want to build with Tess, but there's only one way to find out.

VETERAN
K9
TEAM
REPORTING
FOR DUTY

Chapter 10
Tess

Walking across the dance floor with my phone in my hand, my eyes are on the unanswered texts with Logan when I bounce off a wall of unmoving muscle. My phone flies out of my hand and slides across the wooden dance floor to stop underneath a steel tipped cowboy boot.

Denny wraps his hands around my shoulders to steady me. "You okay, Tess?"

"Shit." I mumble when I see the smashed screen in Larry's hand.

"Sorry darlin'." He smiles apologetically and hands me the tattered remains of my phone. Even if the screen wasn't dark, I know it's dead to me. Shit, I really can't afford to replace it right now, but being unreachable when Logan finally calls is not an option. It's not like him to go more than an hour without returning my text or call, but he hasn't replied to me since lunch.

And now I'm not only without a phone, but without his number.

I mean, who memorizes phone numbers anymore?

"It was my fault." I sigh and bring my eyes up to Denny's. "Can you let Dawn know I ran out to my car and I'll be back in a few minutes?"

"Sure."

I head out the back door into the employee parking lot and fish my keys out of my pocket. Tomorrow I will run to my wireless carrier, buy the cheapest phone they have, and have them restore my contacts from the cloud before calling Logan and apologizing profusely—that is, if he's bothered to call me before then.

Why hasn't he called?

"The thing I liked best about you, besides how you look on my arm, was how I could always count on you to be a money grubbing slut." Dave walks out of the shadows with what looks like a stick in his hand.

My fist clenches around my keys as I turn to face him. "What the hell are you doing here?"

He ignores me and continues with his tantrum. "I figured an Army grunt wouldn't have a pot to piss in, and no matter how good the dick, eventually you'd come back to me because I can give you a future plush with cash and comfort."

I roll my eyes and turn to walk away, unthreatened by him. "You're not allowed here and you know that. If Denny or Max catch you on the property—"

Dave jumps in front of me, backing me up against my car with his size. I jolt as he slams down the stick, which is actually a rolled-up magazine, on the hood of my Xterra. "I should have known the Army grunt was an undercover billionaire. You have a talent for sniffing money out—just like your gold digging whore of a mother."

His words sting, but I refuse to give him the satisfaction of a reaction. "What are you talking about?"

"Look!" He slams his hand down on the page. "He's a fucking Mejer. Hollywood royalty. I guess you hit the jackpot."

"Fuck you." I sneer, my eyes glancing over the picture. The headline says, "Has the prodigal son returned?" In the snapshot, there's a blond guy walking out of a club with Knox and Selyne Mejer wearing sunglasses and a lightweight leather jacket. It could be anyone. And yet the rugged set of his jaw twists my gut.

Could that be Logan?

Why wouldn't he tell me?

I think back to all of our vague conversations about his time in California with his family. Is this what he didn't want to tell me? Is it because he thinks I'm a gold digger, too?

I've heard the term too many times over my life. My mother has always attracted men with money—she works at an art gallery, so only people with means go there—but she's no more of a gold digger than I am. If she was, she would have married any of the ones that asked and made our lives infinitely easier. The rich girls in high school bullied me because, too often, my mother dated one of their fathers or uncles or whatever. Didn't matter that their parents were separated or divorced. They did not welcome my white trash ass at the country club, even when I was physically in attendance. They couldn't talk shit about me in front of their families, so they'd wait until we were at school—spreading rumors about me and my mother.

"So that's it? You're dumping me for a guy with deeper pockets." Dave says in his soft, *I'm a victim,* voice.

"No asshole. I dumped you two months ago because you were fucking a bunch of other women while we were supposedly engaged. Plus, I never wanted to marry you, but you didn't care. You've never cared about who I am or what I want." I lower my head and almost feel sorry for him. "You don't really want me, Dave. You never did. It's the idea of me you want, and I have never been and will never be that girl."

His eyes go over my head, like he's searching the darkness for an answer. Then he shocks me by wrapping his hands around my head and claiming my lips. I'm so surprised, it takes me a second to wedge my hands between us and push him back before I slap him across the face. "What the fuck are you doing?"

"He's putting on a show." A voice comes from behind me. I know it's Logan, but I can't believe he's here. "For me."

"Logan?" I turn my head, my body trapped between the fender and Dave, who has bracketed my body with his arms.

"Hey babe." Logan's tone is soft when talking to me, but his eyes are hard as he comes within reach. He turns his attention to Dave, his voice dropping an octave with a rough edge I've never heard before. "You're going to want to back away from her."

"Or what?" Dave sneers and presses the full length of his body against mine. "Touch me, and I'll sue you."

I cough in surprise and push against his chest again. This blatant aggression isn't like him, and for the first time, he's an unmoving wall. "Oh my god. You're such a fucking pansy, Dave."

"And you're a fucking whore," he hisses.

Logan moves fast. Before I can comprehend what's happening, his body is in front of mine and Dave's on his ass, looking up at us from the ground.

"Tess?" Denny calls from the back door, his eyes narrowing in on us in the darkness. "Shit. We got a situation back here," he says into his earpiece as he breaks into a run.

"It's okay, Denny. Dave was just leaving." I hold my hands up to slow him down. Denny is an absolute bear of a man—ex-military like the owner, Max—and the type to handle business first and ask questions afterward, which is why he's head of security.

Denny's eyes slide from Dave to Logan. "Who the fuck are you?"

"This is Logan," I answer for him.

Dave picks himself off the ground, his lips curled in disgust. "I was done with you, anyway."

"Get your ass out of here or I'll escort you off the property myself." Denny crosses his arms over his chest, the threat of violence lingering in the air. Anyone who works here knows what that means. Security doesn't allow fights on the property, but off property is no holds barred type of combat. Max beat the crap out of four guys "off property" two years ago because he was having a bad night and needed to let off some steam.

No one with an ounce of self-preservation wants to go off property with one of the security guys from the Last Stand.

"Inside, Tess." Denny takes a step back, his eyes on Logan.

"We need a minute." Logan moves to my side and reaches down to interlace his fingers with mine. I'm taken aback by how controlled he is considering the situation. It's almost eerie, the level of calm he's rocking right now.

Denny shakes his head. "No offense, man, but I don't know you, and I'm not leaving Tess out here. You want to talk, bring him inside." He motions to the back door, wordless demanding we precede him inside.

I grab the magazine off the hood of my vehicle and tighten my fingers with his. "Come on, Logan. Denny isn't going to budge on this."

We walk through the employee entrance, and I pull Logan into our locker room. "Can you tell Dawn I'll be out in ten minutes?"

Denny glances at his watch and frowns, his eyes coming back to Logan. "Leave this door unlocked."

I close the door and spin into Logan's arms. My questions about who he really is are secondary to my overwhelming happiness at seeing him again. "What are you doing here?"

"Surprising you, babe." Logan buries his face into my neck, his hands sliding down to cup my ass and pulls my body flush with his. "Thank god I rolled up when I did. What the hell was going on?"

"Are you mad?"

"At you? No. At him? I'm absolutely livid."

"Really? You're so calm."

Logan kisses my neck and then pulls back to look me in the eye. The firm set of his jaw is practiced, but the spark in his green eyes shows me the fire simmering within. "I have a lot of practice blanking out my expressions."

"Because you never know when the paparazzi will snap a photo of you?"

It's true. I can tell by the ways his smile falls. "Why would you say that?"

I pull out of his arms and unroll the magazine to show the picture Dave shoved in my face minutes ago. "It's you, isn't it?"

He sighs and nods reluctantly. "Yeah, that's me. I was going to tell you this weekend."

"Why this weekend? Why not anytime over the last three weeks, or on the night we met?" My insecurities bubble to the surface and I shake my head, wishing them away.

Stupid fucking Dave and his big mouth. I know better than to take anything he says to heart. We went to high school together, so he knows all the right buttons to push to trigger the mean girl memories after all of these years.

"I've been hiding it for years, babe, keeping my name and face as far away from the family as possible while serving my country." He slides his fingers through his military cropped blond hair that is longer than the last time I saw him. "All of our last names are Mejer-Pratt, but my siblings dropped the Pratt, and I dropped the Mejer. I just want to live a normal life—make friends and build relationships based on who I am versus who I'm related to."

"Oh."

"Tell me you understand."

"I understand." I bite my lip, the need to say my piece overwhelming. "Just so you know, I'm not interested in you because of money."

He chuckles. "Well, that's good because right now I don't have any. At least, not the kind of money I should have."

I sag in relief. I don't know why, but that makes me feel so much better. Money is great and all, and someday I want to have lots of it, but I'm tired of having my motives questioned by those who have it when they're usually the ones using it to get what they want—not vice versa.

For Dave to call me a money grubbing slut when he's thrown money at every problem he's ever created is really the pot calling the kettle, and yet he'll never see it that way.

I wrap my arms around Logan and peer up at him with a sweet smile. "If you need a place to stay, you can crash with me. Things seem to be going well with Steve, so my mom is rarely home, and for some reason, she adores you. I'm not exactly sure why, but she asks about you all the time, and she's the one that suggested you stay with us while looking for your own place."

"So you're saying I didn't need to get us a hotel room tonight?" He presses his forehead against mine with a big smile on his face.

I grin back. "For our first night together, a hotel room would be nice."

Logan presses his lips to mine and with one swipe of his tongue, I'm melting in his arms. This kiss is weeks in the making, and so much better than how I remember. He slides his hands under my ass and pulls me tight against him. The evidence of how much he wants me presses against my belly, stoking my need and inciting my desire. Touching and tasting him, having him fill me over and over again—stroke after stroke—has been a fantasy every night since he left me in a post-orgasmic haze leaning against my kitchen island.

Our chemistry is electric, but he's been a total gentleman long distance. While he reminds me how he can't wait to hold me—touch and taste me—daily, he hasn't pushed for cybersex or nude photos. He hasn't even sent me the dreaded dick pic—which, in his case I would welcome. I already know how talented he is with his tongue, and I'm desperate to experience the rest of him.

A heavy knock smacks against the door, breaking us out of the sensual fog enveloping us.

"I'm coming in," Crystal calls from the other side.

Logan sighs and releases me at the same time the door swings open. "I guess I should let you get to work."

Crystal, one of our waitresses, comes in with her hand over her eyes, her fingers strategically splayed to stop her from seeing nothing. "Sorry chick, but we are backed up out there and need you."

"You're not leaving, are you?" I interlace my fingers with Logan's and walk toward the door. "Because I don't have my phone."

"Nope. The guys from the center are meeting me here, and we're hanging out until you get off work."

"Perfect." I turn quickly and kiss his lips before letting go of his hand and ducking behind the bar. Luckily, all the VKC guys are lined up at the end, as if they knew it was my side to tend.

Thursday nights get insanely busy between nine and ten, as ladies get in free and drinks are half price until eleven. So I'm quickly caught up in work, filling drink orders and sneaking glances at Logan as he chats with his friends.

They have a family vibe, and it's one that I can't wait to become a part of.

VETERAN
K9
TEAM
REPORTING
FOR DUTY

Chapter 11
Logan

Finally, it's last call and I'm itching to pull my woman into my arms, claim her lips for all to see, and then whisk her away for the night I've been promising for nearly a month. Watching her flirt with her regulars who all think she hangs the sun and the moon should make me jealous, but I understand playing a role —my sister does the same thing for the cameras—and I know these guys don't stand a chance.

She proves that to me every time she flashes them a smile, but her eyes come to me.

Fuck—she's absolutely perfect. Beautiful, charismatic, and sweet, her customers absolutely love her, especially the old timers.

Tess stops in front of me as Karden slips on his jacket and throws us a mock salute goodbye. The other guys and their women left a couple of hours ago, and Janey tapped out around midnight after dancing a couple rounds with Larry, who has to be around seventy and is more spry than most forty-year-olds I know. "Can I get you anything else, handsome?"

"I'd ask for your phone number, but something tells me you'd say no." I grin.

"My phone is busted, anyway. I guess you'll have to take me home with you instead." She flashes me a flirty smile.

"I can do that." I lean over the bar and meet her halfway, kissing her chastely. "How long until you can leave?"

"I just need to close out my register—"

Her fellow bartender, Dawn, hip-checks her and smiles at me. "—and then she is all yours, pretty boy."

All mine. "Exactly what I want to hear."

Ten minutes later, we're walking hand in hand under the cover of darkness and dimming neon lights. "Are you okay with leaving your car here?"

Tess turns into my chest and slides her fingertips into my waistband, lifting on her tiptoes to press her lips to mine. "Yes, and I called my mom earlier from the bar. Thank god, I actually know her phone number. She's taking care of Brit, so we have all night to ourselves."

I pull open the passenger door of my rental and flex my fingers against her hip. "Get your sexy ass in the car, babe. I've waited long enough to prove how good we can be together."

She smiles and slips into the seat, her grin lasting the ten-mile drive to our hotel. We exit the car in silence, the thrum of anticipation charging the air between us as we walk through the empty lobby to the elevators. As soon as the doors close, I have her in my arms, her body pulled tight against me as I lean my back into the corner and claim her mouth as mine.

Finally mine.

Tess climbs my body, and I have no choice but to slide my hands under her ass and lift until she wraps her legs around my waist. The elevator dings, and I carry her down the hallway to our room, her tongue sweet liquor I'm instantly drunk on.

I knew her taste was addictive, but I didn't realize that I'm a junkie who forgot he can't survive without his fix.

Now that I remember, I'll never be the same.

"I missed you so much," Tess pants, peppering my jaw with kisses as I wrestle with the electronic key card. Finally, I kick the door open and let it shut behind us, bypassing the roses and view of the city to carry her straight to the bedroom.

"I missed you too, babe." I sink to my ass and lie back with Tess draped over my chest. My hands slide up the outsides of her thighs and under her T-shirt, pulling it up and over her head. She's got the curves of a centerfold, her bra molding her breasts into two perfect handfuls and drool-worthy cleavage. I palm the cups and tuck my chin, running my tongue along the seam and up her throat until I'm once again locking lips with her. "You are so goddamn sexy."

"Get naked with me, Logan. I've been fantasizing about touching and tasting you for a month." Tess shimmies down my body and pushes at my T-shirt before unbuckling my belt.

I sit up and pull off my shirt, sucking in my breath as she wraps her fingers around my shaft and pulls my cock out of my shorts.

"Wow." She licks her lips. "I've been wondering what you were saving for me in here."

"I have more than enough for you, and you're going to take everything I have to give you and more. Aren't you, babe?"

She smiles and looks up at me through her lashes as she slowly runs her tongue up the underside of my shaft. I shudder, leaning back on my elbows to watch as my woman wraps her perfect lips around the head and coats my cock in her saliva. Tess takes me as deep as she can, her fingers wrapped around the base as she works me with utter perfection.

It's been a long time since anything other than my hand has worked me, and the pleasure builds in my balls faster than I'd like. "Slow down, babe. You keep sucking on me like that and I'm going to come down your throat."

Tess doubles down, taking me faster and deeper in her warm, wet mouth while pumping my shaft with one hand and kneading my balls with the other. I spread my fingers and push her hair back from her face, the sight of her choking on my cock taking me over the edge.

"Oh, fuck," I groan, my fist wrapping around strands of her hair while my hips come up to fuck her pretty lips as I shoot my cum deep down her throat.

My girl drinks it down, swallowing every drop and sucking me dry.

I pull her off me and roll her to her back, kissing her hard and sliding my hand up the inside of her thighs and underneath her denim skirt. When I saw her wearing it tonight while backed up against the hood of her vehicle, I saw red. Although I always control the rage simmering within, what I really wanted to do was throw Dave against the nearest car and pin him to it, raining my fists down on his face until I was too tired to swing. But he said the magic words right out of the gate—*I'll sue.*

Yeah, the exact reason I stopped fighting once my mom sent me away to the Academy.

Privileged kids sue—fighting with lawyers versus fists —and that's the kind of trouble and publicity I don't need in my life.

Working my way down Tess's body, I pull her skirt off her hips and press a kiss against her silk-covered pussy. "I've been jerking off to your taste for weeks."

"Poor baby," she coos and runs her fingers along my scalp and through the longer strands growing in on top. I haven't had a haircut since before Thanksgiving, prepping for my eventual exit from the military, and although she hasn't said a thing about it, I'm thinking she likes it.

"I'll be okay. We only have another two weeks," I say from between her thighs after I've stripped her bare.

"Two weeks?" Tess lifts her head, her brow furrowed as she stares down at me.

"Yeah, babe. I have enough leave to out-process a few weeks earlier than my ETS date, and with the holiday, my commanding officer signed off on letting me leave the area. My last day is the twenty-second. I'll be here later that evening. Next week, I'll move out of my apartment and have all my shit put in storage while I find a place to live here." I flash her a smile and then stick my tongue out, running it languidly up her center. "What do you say? You want to go house-hunting with me for the holidays?"

Her lips part on a gasp as she nods her head in an unconvincing agreement. "Yes."

"Are you sure?" I continue to tease her, touching her lightly while avoiding the plump clit that is desperate for my attention.

Tess wiggles and spreads her thighs wide, her fingers pressing more insistently against the back of my head. "Yes."

I chuckle against her thigh, my torturous tease causing a fit.

"Please, Logan."

"You want my tongue on you, babe?" Using my thumbs, I spread her lips open, her cunt glistening and clit begging to be plucked.

"God, yes."

"What else do you want?"

"I want everything."

"And I want to give you everything—today, tomorrow, and every day in our future. Whatever you want or need, all you have to do is tell me, and I'll do everything in my power to give it to you," I say between kisses against her thigh.

"I want you to make me come, Logan."

"I can do that, too." I latch on to her clit, sucking it against my teeth in quick pulses. Her thighs tighten around my head as she rolls her hips and rubs her pussy against my face. There's two days' worth of scruff on my chin, which I use to my advantage, scraping my jaw along her sensitive skin. Like the first time, it takes minutes to bring her to the edge, and I'm extremely pleased with how well she responds to my touch.

"Are you ready to come for me, babe?"

"No," she pants.

I slide two fingers inside, her cunt clamping down to milk my digits as her release spills over. Pleased with myself, I lap at the juices dripping out of her, the intoxicating flavor feeding my addiction. "Liar."

Tess whimpers, unclasping her bra and sliding it down her arms before flinging it to the side. "I wanted to come on your cock, not your fingers. I was trying to hold back."

Standing up, I finished disrobing by kicking off my boots and yanking off my jeans and boxers. I wrap my fingers around my hardening cock, stroking as I stare down at her spread out on top of the king-size bed. Her near black hair is spread out like a crown against the stark white comforter, while her plump lips and lusty eyes entice me to bury myself deep inside her and never leave her side again.

"I plan on you coming on my fingers, tongue, lips, and cock tonight, babe. Once won't be enough for me, and it shouldn't be enough for you."

Her eyes follow my hand, and she seductively licks her lips. "Are you saying I should demand orgasms from you?"

Nodding, I smile down at her. "All the pleasure and love I can give—and more."

She crooks her finger with a challenging brow raised. "Fuck me, Logan."

I tilt my head toward the door. "I bought condoms. They are in the other room. Do you want me to go get them?"

Tess bites her lip. "Do you normally use them?"

"I haven't had sex in over a year, since before my last deployment, but yes, I normally use them."

"I made Dave use them, too—because I was positive he was fucking around—even though I am on the pill."

I put a knee on the bed and lean over her, pressing down on the mattress and bracketing her shoulders with my hands. Sucking her pert nipple into my mouth, I bite hard enough to make her flinch and moan underneath me. "I'd prefer there to be nothing between us, considering I want you to be the last woman to soak my cock, but if you want condoms in the interim, I have them."

"Interim?" She scrapes her nails against my scalp and pulls me against her, letting me know how much pleasure she derives from the nipple play.

"Between now and when we live together."

She giggles, wrapping her leg around my waist and pulling my hips down between her splayed thighs. "Remember when I said you were a lot?"

"Yeah?"

"I love that about you." Tess lifts her hips, rubbing her wet slit against my cock. "Now, make love to me."

Staring deep into her eyes, I shift my hip until I'm perfectly aligned and slide forward, penetrating my angel slowly, savoring each fraction of an inch as her arousal lubricates my cock.

Tess's eyes flutter closed as her lips part on a moan. "Oh fuck, that feels good."

"Yeah, you do, babe." Pleasure ripples through my limbs and seeps into my brain. I can't remember anything or anyone ever feeling so good or so right.

Staring down at her, watching ecstasy dance across her face, I know she feels it, too.

She's the one.

My ride or die.

And I'm never letting her go.

Tess opens her eyes and smiles sweetly while sliding her fingers up my biceps. "Kiss me."

Using my forearms, I hook her knees and spread her wide, pinning them near her ears. I drive deeper, my cock kicking with my need to come as I lazily explore her mouth with my tongue, attempting to last as long as possible. "We fit perfectly."

"Yes—" she gasps as the head of my cock slides past her g-spot "—oh god. Yes! Right there."

"Are you ready to come for me again?" I murmur against the softness of her neck, my thrusts slow and steady as her need to release builds. With every stroke, her pussy gets tighter, her walls thickening and making it near impossible for me to not pump my hips, chase my own release, and shoot my seed deep inside of her.

The idea of marking her inside and out is foreign, yet strong. I've never felt anything like it with anyone I've dated in the past.

In this moment, it's like they never existed.

"Please, Logan. I'm so close," she whimpers.

Instinct takes over as I quicken my pace, sending her over the edge at the same time my balls tighten up and I paint her cunt in cum. A half groan/half guttural growl rips from my throat as I bury my face in her neck. "Fuck."

Tess digs her fingernails into my shoulders, her pussy pulsating, my cock jerking its release. Panting, she presses kisses against my shoulder. "My thoughts exactly."

I bring my head up and stare into her gray eyes, darker with sexual satisfaction. "I know I've said it from the moment we met, but you are it for me, babe. Others might covet what's mine, but no one will ever take you from me, because I'll make sure you never want to leave."

Her face softens as she thinks through my bold proclamation, and I can almost hear her protests. She has some deep-seated trauma with money and men who use it to lord over others, but I'm not that guy and never will be. I can be possessive of her without diminishing her role in her own life or our relationship.

"How will you do that?" she whispers, as if she doesn't want to ruin this moment but needs to know.

I caress her cheek with my thumb and smile. "By supplying you with everything I have to give you, to include the independence and freedom to be your own person. I don't want to dim your light. I only want to stand beside you as you build and celebrate your successes."

Tess wrinkles her nose. "What successes?"

"Whatever you want, babe." I shrug. "Dog bakery owner. Entrepreneur. Boss Babe. Mother. Wife. President. I don't care. Whatever you want to do, I'm here to support—" I grin "—because you are mine."

"You realize that if I'm yours, that makes you mine, too."

"I'm counting on it."

VETERAN
K9
TEAM
REPORTING
FOR DUTY

Chapter 12
Tess

We spent Saturday morning and afternoon exploring each other, taking breaks to shower and eat, only to fall right back into bed, where we got dirty and hungry again. This repeated until late afternoon, when I had no choice but to run home so I could change for work. Sometime in between orgasms—as we laid on the bed recovering—Logan told me more about his family and why he chose a different path from them.

With the way he described his mother, I can't say that I blame him.

His siblings, on the other hand, don't sound too terrible.

Logan hung out at the bar with his buddy Karden while I worked until it was close to last call. Like Friday night, Logan brought me back to the hotel where we made love until the early morning hours. I've never felt so consumed before, as if he's a natural extension of me, a limb I'd be lost without.

Two weeks is nothing, and yet I'm already dreading the upcoming separation. I miss him even though he's lying beside me with his powerful forearm stretched across my stomach and his soft snore vibrating against my neck.

"Love you." I whisper in the predawn darkness, the foreign words rolling easily off my tongue.

Logan's arm tightens, and he pulls me closer, but says nothing. Not that he has to. He's all but declared his love for me and made his feelings well known, not just to me, but to his friends. I'm sure if I need him to say the words, he will without a second thought. This connection between us is kismet, and I feel like everything over the last couple of months happened because we were destined to meet. Even though I had been trying to break up with Dave for almost a year, I never felt compelled to pull the plug on our relationship until I walked in on him with the slutty nurse. Maybe that was because I wasn't supposed to be single until Logan was en route to Spring City.

It sounds hokey, but how else do I explain the love I feel for Logan? It's not like I'm the type of woman who falls in love easily, but with him, it's overwhelming.

Logan stirs, his hand sliding down my stomach and over my hip. "I can feel you thinking."

"I thought you were asleep."

"And I thought I was dreaming," he says as he runs his fingers up the inside of my thighs.

I wantonly spread my legs, tilting my hips and letting his fingers find me wet and ready.

Logan growls, his voice husky with sleep. "I dreamed you said you love me."

My body shudders as his fingers slip inside my pussy, curving perfectly to stroke my g-spot, while his thumb rubs circles around my clit. "What if I did?"

"Look at me, babe."

I turn my head to face him, coming nose to nose with my handsome man who is even sexier with a tousled bed head and three days of stubble darkening his cheeks. His green eyes are near black, yet pierce into me all the same.

"I love you, too," Logan says, and presses a possessive kiss to my lips. I melt into his touch, my orgasm coming quickly as my heart swells with unfettered emotion.

He loves me, and I love him.

Plain and simple.

Love given and accepted freely.

Just like that.

My pussy clamps down on his fingers at the same time I cry out. Logan swallows my moans and shifts between my splayed thighs, replacing his fingers with his impressive cock. One slip of the thick head across my g-spot and a second orgasm hits, harder than the first.

Logan groans, "Fuck, babe. There you go. Come again and again for me."

I wrap my calves around his waist and hook my ankles behind his back, wanting our bodies to fuse as one. Logan uses short, smooth strokes to keep up the incessant rubbing of all my pleasure points, the ecstasy coursing through my body almost too much to take. Everything feels so good that I'm riding high on endorphins, my heart on the verge of exploding with overwhelming emotions.

"I love you, I love you, I love you," I chant, unable to hold back the words from spilling out.

Another orgasm crashes over, or maybe the first one never stopped? At this point I can't tell.

Logan curses softly, his cock jerking as he fills me with his cum. "I love you."

He lies on top of me for a minute, his mouth on my neck, hot breaths tickling my ear, as we both pant for breath. Then he brings his face up and looks me in the eye. "You want to look at houses later?"

His question is so off-topic, I can't help but laugh. "What?"

"You have the day off. Why not go look and see what's available? We'll hit all the open houses and make a day of it." Logan rolls to his back, pulling me with him to drape across his chest.

"If that's how you want to spend the day." I close my eyes with my cheek pressed against his pec. This is how I fell asleep last night, which is surprising considering I don't consider myself much of a snuggler.

"Let's catch a few hours of sleep. Then we'll grab brunch, drive around and check out a couple of houses, and eat dinner somewhere we can catch the game."

I smile. "Are you now a Rangers fan? You're on top of their schedule."

"Anything to make my woman happy." He squeezes me and kisses the top of my head before I fall fast asleep.

A few hours later, the telephone rings. Not his cell phone, but the actual room telephone. Logan grumbles something before rolling away and clearing his throat. "Hello?"

. . .

"Wait. What?"

. . .

"All right. All right. Thanks." He hangs up and pulls his legs off of the bed.

"What's going on?" I sit up, clutching the sheet to my chest.

"Gotta turn on the TV and find my phone." He hands me the remote. "Can you change the channel to Entertainment Television?"

"Sure."

Logan walks his sexy naked ass out of the bedroom, returning a minute later with the room service menu and his phone. His brow is furrowed as he stares down at the screen, his thumb swiping along the smooth glass as he hands me the menu. "Are you hungry?"

I chuckle in disbelief. "Logan?"

"What?" He brings his eyes up, his confusion morphing into understanding. "Oh. Sorry. That was Karden, who got a call from Linc, who got a call from Barron, who was sitting with Betty when her social media feed flooded with alerts of my brother Knox on a live interview this morning talking about the Veteran K9 Center."

He waves his phone. "I missed a dozen calls from Karden, Levi, and my mother. I'm almost afraid to listen to her voicemail."

I pat the mattress and smile. "Do you want to take the calls privately?"

"No." He shakes his head and sits next to me, pushing the button and putting the voicemail from his brother on speaker.

"Hey man. I really wish you would answer your phone. I know this isn't what we discussed on Friday, but the gods gave us an opportunity and Langston, Knox, and I couldn't pass it up. If you absolutely hate it, we'll do damage control, but as of this moment the cat's out of the bag—or maybe I should say the dog is off the leash—and the Mejer Veteran K9 Stunt Academy has been born. Please call me before you do anything else. Love you, Bro."

"Who was that?" I ask at the same time Knox Mejer's face pops up on the screen. We turn up the volume to watch as the female interviewer says, "We're here with Langston and Knox Mejer, director and star of 2025's most anticipated summer blockbuster, *After Sunset*—the follow-up to 2022's smash success *Before Dawn* movie franchise."

"What can you tell us about the next installment of

Eric Slater's story?" the interviewer, a beautiful redhead with long legs and a short skirt, asks. She's wearing a pair of black heels that I would kill myself attempting to walk in.

Langston shrugs. "Well, Stephanie, we don't want to give too much away, but you should know that Levi is desperate to jump out of a helicopter right as it blows up."

A replica of Knox Mejer jumps into the frame, pumps a couple of "rock on" devil's horns at the camera—his tongue out and a crazy smile on his lips—and then jumps back out without saying a word.

"Was that Levi?" It's a dumb question, and I have to assume the answer is yes, but I'm not one to follow celebrity gossip. Of course I know who they are—you'd have to be living in a cave without electricity to not know who Knox and Selyne Mejer are—but I don't know any details about their lives.

Logan shakes his head and sighs. "The one and only."

Knox rolls his eyes and chuckles at his twin. "If Levi gets his way, Slater will do all kinds of death-defying acts in *After Sunset*."

"Sounds like you have a lot of exciting things planned. Will Slater's faithful companion Havoc make another appearance?" Stephanie follows up.

"Havoc and a few new friends," Knox says.

Langston nods. "Did you know there were three dogs that played Havoc in *Before Dawn*? The audience responded so well to the animals, we want to include a few more in the next film. Luckily, we have the inside track within the family."

"What does that mean?" she asks.

Knox smiles. "I'm so glad you asked, Stephanie. While I've played a hero and now a veteran Navy Seal as Eric Slater, we have a baby brother who is a real life military hero. Logan has spent the last six years deploying around the world in the Army to protect US friendly assets, interests, and lives. While deployed, he got close with a group of K9 trainers and their highly trained dogs. As these men and women have exited the military, they set up a center that trains support animals for qualifying veterans with PTSD. It's a cause that means a lot to the Mejer family, but especially to our little brother. Logan has joined their mission now that his military service has come to an end, and after hearing about our need for working dogs, established the Mejer Veteran K9 Stunt Academy."

Stephanie smiles. "There have been rumors about the youngest Mejer son resurfacing—I guess this is him?"

"Yeah. He wanted to do something a little different away from the public eye, taking care of his fellow soldiers while also supporting his family here in Hollywood," Langston says.

"We're so proud of our baby brother!" Levi yells from off camera.

Logan groans and hangs his head. I wrap my arms around him and rest my cheek against his bicep. "That's so sweet."

"This is exactly what I did not want," he mumbles. "Now everyone is going to be up my ass."

"Do you think so?"

Logan looks me in the eye. "You have no idea how relentless the paparazzi can be. I might get lucky and they'll be over me and this story in a week or two, but maybe not. I've been avoiding this very thing for ten years."

Pressing my lips together, I slide my hand in his and squeeze his fingers. "Does it have to be that bad? I mean, what if this brings publicity to the center and helps them raise more money? I know Janey said that the support animal program will be funded by government grants and donations."

"That's true. But controlling the media is a full-time job, and the guys didn't sign up for this. Neither did you, for that matter. You understand that there's a possibility someone with a camera will lurk around every corner when you're with me."

Why is he telling me this? Is he trying to warn me away from life with him? "What do you want me to say?"

"Say you love me and you'll weather the bullshit of being a Mejer with me."

Smiling, I remove his phone from his hand and swing my leg over his hips to straddle his lap. I frame his stubbled cheeks and gently kiss his lips while looking him in the eye. "I love you, Logan. We will deal with whatever comes our way—together."

He slides his hands around my hips and pulls me

tight against his hardening cock while peppering my collarbone with kisses. "My ride or die."

His phone rings again, this time the ringer on full volume. I pull back to give him room, but he counters by pinning my hips in place. With little movement, he adjusts and slides inside me, causing a moan to pass my lips. "Oh."

Nothing diverts his attention as he slowly pumps his hips and slides his cock in and out of me. "I fucking love the way you feel wrapped around me, babe. I love everything about you."

"That's good because I'm not letting you go."

Logan rolls us and puts me on my back. He slides his cock in and pulls my legs up, once again hitting my g-spot perfectly while rubbing my clit until my pussy walls are clamping down around him. He follows me almost immediately, with very little noise and no words spoken between us. It's almost like we needed this connection to remind us that no upcoming drama—regardless of how big or small it ends up being—can break us.

Like he said—I'm his ride or die.

He rolls to my side and pulls my knee up on his hip. I slide my hand over his tight stomach and rest my cheek on his chest.

"I guess I should call Levi back, but first, let's see what my mother has to say." He sighs and grabs his phone, pressing a button or two before a female voice comes through the speaker.

"Well, Logan. I'm not sure if this is real or some stunt you and your brothers cooked up, but you've backed me into a corner, and while I don't understand your commitment to your quote-unquote Army brethren, nor to PTSD support animals, I have been advised that this little venture of yours will garner tons of goodwill and foster a new devoted fanbase. So, I have asked Walter to call you Monday morning to start the first disbursement of your funds. Call me when you get this."

Hearing the dry, emotionless, and—dare I say—heartless tone of his mother breaks my heart and makes me want to wrap Logan up in a protective cocoon of love and affection. While my mother is self-centered, and maybe emotionally immature—especially when I was a kid—she's never been cruel. I've always known that Tracy loved me, even when she was too wrapped up in her own shit to pay attention to me.

I squeeze him tight and rub my face against his chest. "Are you okay?"

He draws in a deep breath and lets it out slowly. "It's nothing new to me, babe. Are you ready to take a shower and hit a couple of open houses?"

Something tells me to drop this and just be here for him. Lifting my head, I plaster on a big smile. "Are we showering together?"

"Of course."

"And will you wash my hair?" I bat my eyes, trying to lighten the mood.

"And every other inch of you."

"Mmmm." I push up and kiss his lips, jumping out of

reach when he moves to grab me and pull me close. "I'll meet you in the shower."

Taking my time, I brush my teeth and hair before turning on the water. In the other room, I can hear Logan talking on the phone—presumably to his brother—and I wonder how this will affect us here in Spring City.

Surely, he has to be exaggerating about the paparazzi. I could see them being like that in L.A., but Spring City? Not even the best quarterback in the league is hounded by cameras away from the stadium.

Not that it matters. Let them come for us. I'm by Logan's side, no matter what.

VETERAN
K9
TEAM

REPORTING
FOR DUTY

Chapter 13
Logan

"What did you think of that place?" I pull over and turn to Tess, who has been unusually quiet since we started cruising through open houses this afternoon. The average price point we've looked at today has been around one point eight million, which is chump change compared to my siblings' homes in Southern California.

"It was beautiful." She shrugs. "They've all been beautiful."

"Then why do I feel like you've hated all of them?"

"Honestly?"

"Of course."

"I can't imagine living in any of them." Tess shakes her head. "They're so big. So open. So spacious. So... clean."

I chuckle. "Of course they are clean. People are trying to sell them. What's really bothering you, babe?"

She sighs. "Would you buy a house like this if it was just you moving here? I mean, if you hadn't met me?"

"Ah. I see." I interlace my fingers with hers, staring down at her smooth skin and short nails. Her ring finger on her left hand is glaringly empty, but considering she was wearing another man's ring two months ago, I can't ask her to wear mine even though it would make me so very happy. "The truth is, if I were moving here alone, I'd probably crash with Karden for a while until I figured out which part of town I wanted to live in. And then, maybe Saint and I would get a house together until either of us got a girlfriend and needed a bit more privacy. Before I met you, I wanted to move here, but I didn't know if I would establish roots here. Because of you, I want to establish a home, not just a place to lay my head. Does that make sense?"

"I guess so." She bites her lip and motions to the houses in the neighborhood, all of which have five or more acres surrounding them. "But I don't need all this to be impressed by you. I'm already hopelessly in love with you."

Fuck, that makes my heart soar, but this isn't about impressing her. It's about our future.

"When you think about the houses we've looked at today, I want you to picture our lives ten years from now." I bring her hand up to my lips and stare into her eyes while painting us a picture. "We're married with two, three, maybe four kids. At least one or two of them are in elementary school—so we'll want to be in a neighborhood with the best schools. Obviously, we'll have a couple of dogs, but maybe we also have a hobby farm with a few ponies, a dozen chickens, a gaggle of goats, and a load of llamas."

"A load of llamas?" She laughs.

"Whatever." I grin. "The point is, I don't want you to look at houses with the next six months in mind, but the next thirty years. You are my roots, babe. From the moment we met, I knew it and so did you. Let's look for our forever home and build all our memories there."

"You really are Hollywood. You just painted me a beautiful cinematic picture."

"Yeah?" I grin.

She nods and closes her eyes. "Tell me more."

"Okay. Imagine the bed we lie in on our first night as man and wife. Then picture the night I put our first child in you. Maybe it's in our bed, or maybe it's in our kitchen while I bend you over the counter, or on top of the pool table in our entertainment room. Then picture the morning you tell me you're pregnant. Or a year later—our child's crib and nursery, then two cribs, then bunk beds, and a swing set, and maybe even a treehouse. Do you want those memories left behind as we outgrow each home and have to move? No. So let's buy our dream home now."

Tess takes in a deep breath, opens her eyes, and shakes her head. "You are a lot, you know that?"

I grin and nod, because I know she sees my point. "Yeah, but you like it."

"I not only like it, I love it."

"Good, but I love you more."

VETERAN
K9
TEAM
REPORTING
FOR DUTY

Epilogue
Logan - Eight Months Later

Levi shakes his head and hands me a tumbler of top shelf whiskey. "I can't believe you're getting married tomorrow."

The whole not rushing to put a ring on Tess's finger went out the window when I moved to town two weeks later. Before New Year, we toured three houses and put an offer on our forever home. Sometime between the inspection and the day we closed—right after Valentine's Day—I drove her out to the property to watch the sunset from the deck off the primary suite. As the giant glowing ball touched the Rocky Mountains, and the sky shifted from blue to orange to pink to purple, I got down on one knee and asked her to be my wife.

Now I'm sitting on the private rooftop of the Overlook Hotel with a view of the city lights. I'm here with my family, Steve the man friend, and the guys from the VKC—to include a couple of men I don't know—friends of friends and security for my A-list celebrity brothers.

We just ate an amazing steak and lobster dinner, and now we're lounging under the stars, drinking and smoking cigars. Well, some of the guys are smoking. I never developed a taste for them, but I like the smell.

There's music playing, a TV broadcasting sports highlights hanging over the outdoor 360 fireplace, a bar, and a couple of pool tables under the glass canopy creating a low-key night, which is exactly what I wanted for my bachelor party.

"What's not to believe?" I clink glasses with Levi. "You've met Tess. She's perfect."

He smiles. "She is pretty great. You got lucky."

"I feel lucky. How about you? Are you still off again, on again with Evangelina?"

Levi bites his cheek and looks off into the distance. "Nah. People say absence makes the heart grow fonder, but that's a crock of shit."

Karden walks up with one of the big guys that I don't know. "Logan, this is my buddy Griffin."

Oh, right. The recently retired Navy Seal who was also one of Karden's foster brothers back in Philly. Apparently, there are a handful of them that all went into the military to break away from their troubled pasts.

I offer him my hand. "Hey man, glad you made it."

"Thanks for letting me crash your party. Congratulations on your impending nuptials." Griffin's voice is gravel, as if he choked down concrete before coming. Or maybe he doesn't talk much. He certainly has that combat veteran look about him—his gaze darting around as if he's clocking his six—uncomfortable with having so many people at his back.

"Will you still be in town tomorrow?" I ask casually, wishing there was something I could do to make him more comfortable.

"Yeah." Griffin accepts a beer from the cocktail server.

"If you have nothing better to do, come to the wedding. The ceremony will be simple and elegant, but the reception should be a wild and crazy time."

"Thanks, man. That's real nice of you to offer."

Langston—who I think has had a couple of drinks because he's the loosest I've ever seen him—taps a knife against his glass. "Gentlemen, we're here to celebrate my brother Logan and his bride-to-be Tess. Little brother, nothing was easy for you, but you never let that stop you from becoming the best version of yourself. Of all of us, really. You deserve to be happy, and you deserve the love of a good woman, both of which you've found. I'm so fucking proud of the things you've accomplished and wish you nothing but continued success. To Logan and Tess!"

Everyone raises their glasses. I return their crystal salute, nod my head, and say my simple thanks. I'm not a big speech person, and I really don't want to give one now, but everyone is staring at me expectantly.

"Fuck, I don't know what to say. Thank you all for being here this weekend. Each one of you means a lot to me. I have my brothers, and I have my brethren, two families born of different blood—one red and one green, as Knox says—but both of which are vital parts of who I am today. It means the world to me to share this weekend with you."

"Fuck yeah!" Levi lifts his glass, and everyone joins in.

I spend the next hour bullshitting with the guys, playing a couple rounds of pool and getting my ass handed to me by Saint and Kemp.

My father comes up and puts his hand on my shoulder, squeezing gently. "I'm very proud of you, Logan. Tess is a truly wonderful woman, and the two of you make a beautiful couple. I especially like the way you are together—hopelessly in love and unafraid to show it."

"Thanks, Dad."

He smiles sadly and sways a little on his feet. Jesus, are both my father and brother drunk? That should make the wedding interesting tomorrow. "I know I wasn't there for you like you needed me to be, and while I have regrets, looking at you here and now, I wouldn't change any of it. Maybe I could have intervened a bit more when things between you and your mother got heated. I could have worked harder to give you safe outlets for your anger. Or I should have fought for you a little harder. But everything you went through turned you into the man you are today, and that I wouldn't change for the world."

I nod, unsure how to respond. "It's all good, Dad."

"You know, your mother loves you..." His voice fades, and I'm thinking we need to get him back to his room, which, thankfully, is in this hotel.

Looking at the assembled party, I lock eyes with Levi

and Knox and imperceptibly tilt my head in our father's direction. Knox nods while Levi grins as the two of them walk toward us.

"Time to wind down, don't you think? Can't show up hungover on your wedding day," Levi says, putting his arm around our father's waist.

We're all staying at the hotel tonight, so they only have to escort him down one flight of stairs to one of the four penthouse suites below. I was worried that Spring City wouldn't have posh enough rooms for my family—specifically my mother—but then they found this place and everything worked out. I guess the owner, some Italian hotelier named Sebastian, remodeled this place two years ago specifically to cater to artists performing at the Universal Theatre down the road.

"I'm proud of all of my boys," our father drones on.

Levi chuckles. "Yeah, time for bed."

Knox stays with me and points out Langston talking to Linc, Karden, and Kemp. "I think he's going to recruit all of your old Army buddies to be extras in our next film. He can't seem to get over the size of Kemp or Karden, and Linc is plain pretty."

I shake my head and laugh. "Yeah. He knows it, too."

"I overheard Bishop say something about losing his best friend in Afghanistan," Knox says low, so only I hear. "Is that—"

"Yeah." I cut him off. "It was me, Saint, Bishop, and Miller on patrol. Karden and his dog Kiki, the Malinois you met yesterday, are the ones that took out the sniper who had us pinned down."

"Fuck." Knox wraps his big hand around the back of my neck. "I'm glad you have these guys, Logan, and they have you. Not that I envy what you've been through, but I do envy the bond you have with these men. It's stronger than any friendship I've ever had in Hollywood, aside from Levi."

"Yeah." My phone buzzes in my pocket, and I'm praying it's Tess. We haven't spent a night apart since I moved to town right before Christmas, and the idea of sleeping in my bed alone tonight kills me.

Who the fuck came up with the bright idea that the bride and groom shouldn't see each other the night before the ceremony?

Not that I had a choice in this matter. My mother and sister whisked her, Tracy, Dawn, Jamie, Betty, Brandi, Mari, Janey, Charity, and Sylvie up to a private club in Denver with six security guys in tow. I begged Selyne to keep it low key and local, but she waved away my concerns and called me a party pooper. Only because Tess told me she had it under control did I relent. I'm well aware of how overbearing and pushy my mother and sister can be. And while it's been over a year since my sister was involved in any kind of scandal, I don't want to think about the trouble she invites while out with my fiancée.

I pull my phone out of my pocket and sigh in relief.

Hey Lover. Do you miss me?

I miss you!!!

Epilogue

Oh shit, I think my bride-to-be is drunk.

I do miss you, babe.

Are you having fun?

Are my mother and sister behaving themselves?

They are… actually, I'm not sure where your mom is. Selyne, Dawn, Betty, Charity, and I were dancing until a few minutes ago.

I'm a sweaty mess.

I'm sure you are still beautiful.

Are you safe?

No. Come get me right now.

What?

I'm kidding. We have six huge guys watching over our every move.

And we're all wearing wigs and glasses.

It's the most ridiculous disguise I've ever seen, but it seems to work because even though everyone is staring at us, no one has approached Selyne.

So that's how my sister planned a fun night out.

Wigs, huh? Send me a picture.

Tess sends me a picture of her in a black, strapless corset dress—one I've never seen before—and a long, lavender wig. She looks beyond sexy, like a succubus that came up from hell to lure her next victim. If she's not getting hit on, it's because security won't let anyone get close enough. A primal desire to find and cover her up hits my gut, but I push it down. I trust my woman, even if I don't trust anyone else.

> You're asking for trouble in that dress, babe.

> Trouble from who, lover?

> Me.

> Maybe I'll sneak into your room tonight when we get back to the Springs.

> Maybe I'll be waiting for you in the private gardens at Castilla's Reserve.

> Do you realize that by this time tomorrow you'll be helping me out of my wedding dress?

> Babe, by this time tomorrow, you'll be Mrs. Tess Mejer-Pratt.

She fills my screen with heart emojis.

> I love you so much, Logan.

> My life feels like a fairytale, and I never thought I would love anyone as much as I love you.

> I love you more, babe.

I finally bring my face up to see Knox staring at me with an amused tilt to his lips. "So that's what head over heels in love looks like."

"No more powerful drug in the world, brother."

It's a little after three thirty and I'm having the attendant fix my bowtie when my father walks in with my brothers. Considering I haven't been super close with them over the years, and I didn't want any hurt feelings, I chose to not have anyone stand up with me. Thankfully, that works fine for Tess, who has a lot of friends, but no true best friend that expects to be her maid-of-honor.

Tracy is walking Tess up the aisle, and I'll take it from there.

"You ready?" Levi smiles. We're all wearing custom-made tuxedos made by Gio Salvatori, a man with an excellent reputation even in the elite circles of A-list celebrities. It surprised me to learn he was the primary tailor for the Scott family who own the Rocky Mountain Rangers football team.

Of course, I met them when Knox came to town during Spring Training, and we got a personal meet and greet with the star quarterback, Declan Scott.

I forgot how far fame and fortune take you, and while it's fun in small doses, I'm happy to not be pulled back into that life.

"I think so."

"I have something for you." My father sets a large gift bag down on the table. "For all of my boys, actually."

He hands each of us a leather wrapped watch box with BVLGARI embossed in gold on the top. I pop it open to find an elegant, yet understated, black-faced watch with gold numerals and a simple black leather band. I note he is also wearing one, and my brothers are all opening the same one. "This is great, Dad. Thanks."

"You should know that your mother is currently gifting Tess and Tracy a necklace that matches ones she bought for her and Selyne."

"Great." I smile and nod, praying that it isn't something Tess hates. I do not want to deal with my mother's passive aggressive attitude if Tess doesn't want to wear the gifted necklace on her big day.

As if my father can read my mind, he puts his hands up. "Don't worry. She's not going to ask Tess to wear it today. She just wanted the four of them to have something that bonded them."

That's actually kind of nice.

An usher pops his head in. "You can take your places, gentlemen."

We're having a smaller wedding, completely private

for obvious reasons, but no less sophisticated than my A-list family expects. Let's be honest, no less luxurious than my mother demands. We've rented out the gardens and the surrounding grounds at Castilla's Reserve, the same ones I texted Tess about last night, and the only way paparazzi could snap a photo of us is if they flew in via helicopter, and even then we have a privacy screen shielding us from the sky above.

I take my place at the altar, greeting Daniel, the officiant who we met six weeks ago, and then looking out at the fifty people in attendance. Karden and Saint give me a chin tilt, while Linc flashes me a thumbs up—and then "I get to love you" by Ruelle plays softly and Tess appears at the end of the aisle with her mother. As soon as I see her, no one else exists. My vision tunnels, and all I see is Tess smiling back at me. Electricity skitters down my spine and jump-starts my heart—a sense of déjà vu reminding me of the first time I saw her.

She's the one.

My future.

My life.

Tess

This morning I woke up with a mild hangover, but my sister-in-law-to-be gave me something that perked me right up. Considering she's from Hollywood, I should have been cautious about taking or drinking anything offered, but I know she wouldn't hurt me because she wouldn't hurt Logan. Actually, I don't think Selyne is capable of hurting anyone. She's remarkably naïve for a twenty-seven-year-old, and yet worldly beyond anything I'll ever understand. So smart in some aspects of her life, and almost childlike in others.

And sweet... she is so stinking sweet. I've gotten more hugs from her in the last forty-eight hours than I have in my life. Not an exaggeration. Well, maybe a little exaggeration, but I've never had a touchy-feely friend like her. She either really likes me and means it when she says she wants us to be as close as sisters can get, or she's an Oscar-winning actress. Considering the family, both of which could be true.

My mom fusses with my hair while I stand in front of the full-length mirror in the bridal suite. "You are so beautiful, baby," Tracy says with tears in her eyes.

"Oh, Mom. Don't start crying or I'll start crying."

Loretta Mejer commissioned the dress I'm wearing. I accepted her gift, even though I worried there would be expectations placed upon me wearing said designer gown. Virtually, we went over many designs together, but even after my first fitting, I expected her to change the design to cover up the tattoos on my shoulders, chest, and arms. The first time we met, she made a backhanded compliment about them, and it's been hanging out there ever since.

Surprisingly, when they delivered the dress this morning, it looked exactly as it did during the final fitting. Illusion, long sleeves with lace appliques that come to my fingertips, an off the shoulder, scalloped neckline, a form-fitting bodice, and a long full skirt that is tailored to let the tips of my heels peek out of the front. The train is barely long enough to drag on the ground, but even Tracy insisted that a flowing skirt was the touch of elegance a wedding requires.

There's a gentle knock on the door before it swings open. Selyne dances her way into the room with her mother trailing at a cautious rate behind her.

My sister-in-law-to-be gasps. "You are gorgeous. Logan is going to lose it. You look just like a rock-n-roll Disney princess."

I giggle and turn back to face my reflection. "I feel like a princess. Thank you, Loretta."

My mother-in-law-to-be stands beside me with a genuine smile on her face. "Thank you for letting me be a part of your special day." She's wearing a dark navy blue skirt suit that has a tuxedo-meets-Chanel vibe to it with shiny lapels and a satin strip run up the sides of the knee-length skirt.

My mother is wearing a designer dress as well—dark blue with intricate beadwork, a deep v in the front and back, and draped sleeves—something that Loretta insisted on buying for her.

And I couldn't even begin to describe how gorgeous Selyne is in a dark blue, form-fitting halter dress with a mermaid skirt and low-cut back.

Loretta sets a Tiffany blue gift bag down on a side table. "I brought you something, but you don't have to wear it today if you don't want to."

I turn my attention to her as she pulls out several large Tiffany necklace boxes, handing one to me, Tracy, and Selyne. "In minutes, you will be part of the family. I know Logan and I don't have the best relationship, but I do love him very much, and I want to welcome you and your mother, and hope that we can establish a special bond despite the distance."

Opening the box, I'm thrilled with the simple platinum chain with three beveled sapphires spaced evenly apart. "This is beautiful."

"I was going to get us matching pearls, because as my mother said, every woman should have a string of pearls, but then I figured where besides a wedding does a modern day woman wear pearls? I thought this was more practical, and I knew you'd prefer platinum over gold to match your wedding ring."

It's then I notice her necklace, which is the same as the one she gifted me. I turn to see my mother and Selyne pulling out the same necklace. Unbidden tears come to my eyes. "Thank you, Loretta. This is so very thoughtful."

"It really is," my mom says as she lifts her hair, and Selyne fastens it in place.

Lifting the necklace out of the box, I hand it back to her. "Will you put it on me?"

Loretta smiles brightly and turns me toward the mirror, standing behind me to fasten it in place. We stare at each other through our reflection, a new understanding forming between us. Not that I'll let my guard down with her, because I've heard enough stories to know that is a dangerous thing to do, but I will give friendship a chance.

Another knock hits the door and a male voice seeps through the open sliver into the room. "Ladies, it's time to take your places."

Selyne claps her hands together. "Showtime!"

Loretta and Selyne precede us out of the room, leaving me and my mother alone.

Tracy chuckles. "Your in-laws are a lot, you know that?"

"Yeah, but I kind of like it. I guess Logan doesn't fall nearly as far from the tree as he thinks."

She grabs my bridal bouquet and interlaces her fingers with mine. "I'm so happy for you, Tess. I didn't give you the best examples of a loving relationship growing up, but I'm glad you found one, anyway."

I squeeze her fingers. "Maybe you can finally let yourself fall head over heels in love, too. I like Steve, and he adores you, and it was nice of him to act as Brit's handler for the wedding."

Because of course Brit had to be in attendance. If we had a wedding party, she would have been our ring bearer. Definitely.

Tracy rolls her eyes but smiles. "Yeah, he's pretty great."

We walk through the threshold, the air thick with gardenia, and stop at the end of the aisle. Logan is standing at the makeshift altar with his hands clasped in front of him, a babbling fountain spraying in the pond behind him. He's breathtakingly handsome in his tuxedo, but it's when his eyes come to me that time stands still. The same jolt I got the night we met hits me square in the belly, and I feel the need to stumble forward as my body becomes absolutely weightless.

My mom squeezes my fingers as the music plays. "You ready?"

"Yeah," I whisper as Logan's lips spread in a wide smile and he throws me one of those flirty winks that make my knees weak. Smiling back, we walk down the aisle and pass the intimate crowd. Honestly, I see no one other than Logan staring back at me. Once at the altar, I turn and accept a hug from my mother before she hugs Logan and takes my bouquet. Then we're standing together, our hands joined, time standing still.

Logan's eyes trace over my body, a held breath escaping from his lips. "You are fucking exquisite, babe— the most beautiful bride there has ever been."

Biting my lip, I have so many things I want to say, but

Daniel the officiant clears his throat and effectively silences me by starting the ceremony.

"Welcome, and on behalf of Logan and Tess, I want to thank you for attending this special day. I've been doing weddings for ten years, and I've met with thousands of couples in that time, and while I only spent a couple of hours with Logan and Tess, the overwhelming love they have for each other left a profound impact on me. I have a standard script I normally work from, making minor tweaks for the couple of the day, but after leaving Logan and Tess's home, I was compelled to write something new." Daniel nods to both of us.

"This is not a religious ceremony, and yet, we spoke at length about fate and the universe conspiring to bring two people together. Without a word spoken, Logan recognized Tess as his future, and in Tess's words, *she felt something, too.*" He curls his fingers in air quotes, which causes a couple of people in the audience to chuckle.

I blush and smile up at Logan, a rogue tear falling from my eye.

Daniel continues. "In their case, things happened at exactly the right time in their lives to open them to meeting their soulmate and starting the rest of their life together. Neither were looking for love. If anything, the timing was terrible. Logan was transitioning from the military and moving to a new state to start a new business venture. Tess had just gotten out of a relationship that would have left most people jaded. But when they met, nothing else mattered. That's when you know it's kismet. That's when you know the universe is talking to you, telling you to wake up and pay attention. I'm thrilled to be here today uniting this beautiful couple in marriage."

The next ten minutes speed by, and the next thing I know, I have a ring on my finger and I'm in Logan's arm.

"Hello Mrs. Mejer-Pratt." Logan leans forward and kisses me sweetly, almost chastely, but that isn't going to work for me.

I throw my arms around his neck and press my body against his, letting everyone know that this is my man. As if the wedding dress and ceremony weren't obvious enough.

Logan chuckles and responds by bending me backwards and laying a lipstick melting kiss on me, leaving me breathless and wanting more. "I love you, babe."

"I love you, husband."

VETERAN
K9
TEAM
REPORTING
FOR DUTY

Second Epilogue
Logan - Five Years Later

"Pulling up to the house now."

"Cool, we'll let you go. Let us know if you can bribe Tess into taking a vacation to Fiji. The whole family will be there. And I need to take chubby cheeks surfing," Levi says.

"There is no way in hell I'm letting you take my three-year-old daughter surfing in Fiji." I put my truck in park and cut the engine.

"Come on, man. I wouldn't take her out on a big wave. Just some chill body surfing."

Shaking my head, I exit my vehicle, open the back-door, and lift Brit from the seat, setting her gently on the ground. Bandit, our five-year-old Boxer, jumps out after her. I put my phone on speaker as we enter the house, making sure Tess is within earshot before responding to Levi. "You know what, man? I'll let you take it up with Tess."

"Awww, man." Levi chuckles.

"Exactly." I flash her a devious grin. "Talk to you later."

"Later, bro."

Tess quirks her brow. "Do I even want to know what that is about?"

I put my phone and wallet down on the counter and walk up behind her as she chops vegetables at the counter for stir-fry tonight, slipping my hands around her swelling belly. She's four months pregnant with our second child, yet she only recently regained her appetite. Cher Vale says each pregnancy is different, and this one was definitely a new ballgame for both of us. "Your favorite brother-in-law wants to take Emma surfing in Fiji."

"Like hell." She scoffs, offering me a slice of bell pepper.

"That's what I said." I pull the slice in with my tongue and the nibble on her fingertips, my hands sliding low on her belly.

Her eyes spark with heat, need, and longing. With an active three-year-old and another on the way, along with the nausea Tess had at the beginning of this pregnancy, we've done nothing more than fall into bed exhausted night after night. I miss my wife, even though she's sleeping beside me. And she's mentioned miss me, too.

She puts the knife down and turns, wrapping her arms around my neck. "You know, Grandma Tracy offered to take Emma for the weekend."

"Has she?" I lean my forehead against hers and give

her a chaste kiss while sliding my hands low to cup her ass.

"Friday through Sunday. Two whole nights and one full day of nakedness."

"Do we trust Grandma Tracy to last an entire weekend?" I tease. While Tracy might not have been a reliable mother, she's been an excellent grandmother. Of course, she has help.

"Even if I didn't trust her, I trust Steve. The man is more maternal than either of us." Tess lifts on her toes and puts her lips over mine. "What do you say, handsome? Do you want to spend the weekend naked with me?"

"You plan Emma's weekend with your mother. I'll plan our naked time." Flexing my fingers against her ass, I'm seconds away from lifting and setting her on the counter when our daughter comes running into the room with Brit beside her.

"Daddy's home!"

"Yeah, I am." I let go of Tess and turn in time to catch my daughter throwing herself at my legs.

I swear, she learned that from Selyne.

Or Levi.

Or maybe both.

Jump first and worry about the consequences later— that's my girl. It's not that I don't trust Levi to take care of my daughter... I don't trust Emma.

The girl has no fear.

No sense of preservation or survival.

She is 50% Levi daredevil, and 50% Selyne optimism.

Everything will work itself out.

"How was your day?" Emma asks me, her chubby and filthy fingers pressing against my cheeks.

"My day was good, princess. How was yours?" I grab another slice of bell pepper off the chopping block and feed half of it to her, popping the other half in my mouth.

"Did you make another movie today?" She asks.

"Not today, but your uncles Knox and Levi are going to Fiji next month and Linc is meeting them there with Lazarus."

"Can we go?" My daughter beams. She loves all the dogs, and her uncles, and pretty much thinks the world revolves around her. I guess she is more like Selyne than I thought.

"Mommy and I are going to look at our schedules and talk about it this weekend. Okay?"

"Okay." She sighs.

"Speaking of this weekend," Tess interjects, "how would you like to spend it at grandma's house?"

"Yay! But who will feed the goats?"

"I'm sure we can take care of it." Tess chuckles.

"Okay, but make sure you give them the right bottles. They're very picky." Emma dramatically repeats what she's heard both Tess and I joke about when feeding our growing hobby farm full of animals, and glances at the vegetables on the counter. "Can I have another one?"

I set her down and hand her another bell pepper strip. "Why don't you go wash your hands and your face, and then we'll sit down to dinner."

"Okay." She runs off with Brit and Bandit on her tail.

They are excellent babysitters, as well as superb beggars, and they know a three-year-old attention span equals lots of forgotten treats.

I press a kiss to Tess's forehead and inhale her shampoo. "Fuck, I can't wait until tomorrow night."

She tosses the vegetables into the wok and then wipes her hands before turning into me and cupping my semi-hard cock with her palm. "I can wait either."

It's Friday afternoon, and I'm closing the office early so I can get home before Tess is back from dropping Emma off at her mother's. From the day my brothers announced the Mejer Veteran K9 Stunt Academy, the phones have been ringing. Within the first month of bookings, I technically didn't need my trust fund to invest in the VKC, as I had a line of Hollywood investors begging me and Janey to donate and invest in our respective businesses. Of course, Janey wants to hold the center close to her and her fellow veteran's hearts, and I don't blame her.

We did, however, accept over five hundred grand in donations, which set us up to train and home twenty-five PTSD service animals with combat veterans over the last few years. And since then, we haven't had to pay out of pocket for one service animal, because we have a waiting list of sponsors.

When I'm not handling business, I'm restocking

Tess's bakery case inside the Pet Plaza, which is what we call the new storefront of the Veteran K9 Center. Toys, leashes, treats, grooming, and veterinary services run out of that building, although the veterinarian—who also happens to be an Army veteran—wants to expand her business to include a surgical suite. We're negotiating the lease of a new building on the property with her now because we don't want to lose her.

Yeah, we have a good thing going on out there.

I pull into the garage and let Brit and Bandit out of the backseat. We enter the house, and although I thought I was coming home early to beat Tess to the romantic stuff, I find a bottle of Prosecco and a plate of chocolate-covered strawberries on the counter, and something mouthwatering warming in the oven. I set down the two dozen roses I picked up on the way home and peek at the note next to the strawberries.

Hello Lover.

I'll be home by four, and I'm hoping you are naked and waiting for me when I get there.

Grabbing two vases off the top shelf, I make quick work of the roses and carry one bouquet up with me to our bedroom. There, I quickly shed my clothes, noting Tess pulled out some of my favorite lingerie and laid it out on the bed. Not that I think she'll have time to put any of it on. I plan on pulling her into my arms as soon as she crosses the threshold.

I jump into the shower and rinse off the dog slobber from earlier, a hazard of the job, and turn the water off in time to see Tess walking into the bathroom while pulling her dress up and over her head. Grinning, I open the glass door and coax her forward with the crook of my finger.

"I'm not too late, am I?"

I turn the hot water back on and pull her under the spray. "You are right on time, babe."

Tess wraps her arms around my waist and sighs, her bare skin touching mine, firing all of my nerve endings and heightening my desire. "Fuck, I missed you."

Kissing the top of her head, I slide my hands up and down her back. "I missed you, too. Emma all settled with grandma?"

"Yes."

"Want me to wash your hair?"

She presses her lips against my chest and nods her head.

"And then, how about I give you a massage?" I ask at the same time as I grab the bottle and squeeze out a quarter-sized dollop of shampoo. Running my fingers through her wet strands and massaging her scalp, Tess lets out a low moan, and then takes a step back to sit on the built-in bench. I follow her without speaking a word, continuing the head massage. I grab the hand-held and rinse her hair, but when I turn to grab the conditioner, she's sliding her hands up my thighs and fisting my cock.

"How about I massage your head while you massage

mine?" Tess looks up at me through her lashes, drops of water flinging off them with every blink.

A low groan escapes as she parts her lips and takes me deep. "Ah, fuck yeah."

It takes me a good thirty seconds to remember what I was doing before this amazing woman took me in hand. I grab the conditioner and lather her hair, my fingers flexing against the back of her neck when she quickens her pace and takes me deep, gagging ever so slightly before pulling back. "God damn, babe. That feels fucking amazing."

Tess looks up at me while swirling her tongue around the sensitive head. "It tastes amazing, too."

"Stand up and turn around."

She presses a kiss to the tip and stands, turning coyly while staring at me from over her shoulder. "Are you going to fuck me now, husband?"

"Brace yourself, babe." I say as I slide the head of my cock up and down the slit of her hot pussy. Tess bends over and arches her back, her feet spread and hands on the bench. I slip inside of her, and both of us moan in unison.

"Oh god. You feel so good. I want to cry." Tess whimpers and tosses her hair back.

"We have all weekend, and I think we need to take the edge off." I say at the same time as I pump my hips faster and grind my cock against her g-spot. "Play with your clit, babe. Come for me."

One thing about Tess when she's pregnant, her clit is even more sensitive than usual—and I never had a problem getting her off before. It takes less than sixty seconds for her pussy to convulse around my cock with her climax, which sends me sky-rocketing over the edge. I pump my hips as my cock jerks to completion and then lean forward and press kisses to her back when I'm depleted.

Slipping out of her, I turn and pull her under the rain head above our heads, rinsing the last of the conditioner out of her long, lush, dark waves. We quickly clean ourselves up, turn off the water, and climb into bed to hold each other in uninterrupted bliss.

"I love you so much, babe." I say with a content sigh while stroking her damp hair. "You make me happier than I ever dreamed I could be."

Tess lifts her head from my chest and turns to look me in the eye. "You said it the night we met. I'm the one you were waiting for."

I chuckle and narrow my eyes. "Actually, I think I said I was the man YOU were waiting for."

"Still cocky as ever." She teases with a smile.

"No cocky, but confident that we are perfect together, babe."

"You are still a lot, but I love it." She pushes up and presses her lips to mine. "And you."

Coming next: Bishop and Charity in Mine to Worship

Want more of the Mejer family? Subscribe to my newsletter to get the latest information on the Hollywood Lights Series coming in mid 2024.

The crew at the Last Stand: Dawn, Corey, Denny, Max, and more, have their own books. Check out the series, Last Stand Saloon

Jamie and Kirian also have their own story: Puppy Love, which is part of the Animal Attraction series

Most of my books take place in Spring City, Colorado and feature cameo appearances from characters in past / present / and sometimes future books from all of my series. Check out my website for a cross-over / series map.

Also by Kameron Claire

Want more **Witty** Tongues, **Wicked** Needs, & **Wild** Deeds?

<u>Hollywood Lights (Pre-Order)</u>

* Billionaire Romance *

Show Time (Securing Selyne)

Money Shot

Three Shot

Martini Shot

Long Shot

<u>Veteran K9 Team</u>

* *Military Romance* *

Mine to Cherish

Mine to Crave

Mine to Possess

Mine to Adore

Mine to Covet

Mine to Worship

Mine to Protect

Mine to Treasure

Hot Nights with the Boss

** Forbidden Office / Age-Gap Romances **

Dating the Boss

Flirting with the Boss

Teasing the Boss

Tempting the Boss

Rangers Football

** Sports Romance **

Play Action Fake

Quarterback Sneak

Personal Foul

Two-Point Conversion

Red Zone

Man to Man Coverage

Short Story Collections and Bundles

Animal Attraction 4-Story Collection

Vegas Nights 4-Story Collection

Last Stand Saloon 4-Story Collection

Instalove Bundle

Grayson Enterprises Series

Bedding the Boss

Enticing the Ex

Tempting the Teacher

Wedding the Widow

About the Author

 USA Today Bestselling Author Kameron Claire writes stories with witty tongues, wicked needs, and wild deeds. Her books emphasize strong female leads and the protective alpha males who know how to love and support kick-ass, take-charge women. Many of her books contain military veterans, boss babes, gentle but dominant men, and goofy K9 hijinks.

Find her everywhere via linktr.ee/kameronclaire
Signed Paperbacks and discounted eBook bundles are available exclusively on her store
Subscribe to the Witty, Wicked & Wild community and read all her books online for as little as $5 a month.

www.ingramcontent.com/pod-product-compliance
Lightning Source LLC
Chambersburg PA
CBHW031600310726
48974CB00003B/753